The
Taking
of
MARIASBURG

Also by JULIAN F. THOMPSON

Simon Pure
A Band of Angels
Discontinued
Facing It
A Question of Survival
The Grounding of Group 6

The
Taking
of
MARIASBURG

Julian F.
Thompson

**SCHOLASTIC
HARDCOVER**

Scholastic Inc.
New York

Copyright © 1988 by Julian F. Thompson.
All rights reserved. Published by Scholastic Inc.
SCHOLASTIC HARDCOVER is a registered trademark of Scholastic Inc.

No part of this publication may be reproduced in whole or in part, or stored in a retrieval system, or transmitted in any form or by any means, electronic, mechanical, photocopying, recording, or otherwise, without written permission of the publisher. For information regarding permission, write to Scholastic Inc., 730 Broadway, New York, NY 10003.

Library of Congress Cataloging-in-Publication Data

Thompson, Julian F.
The taking of Mariasburg.

Summary: When she inherits a large sum of money from the father that she never met, seventeen-year-old Maria decides to start a town that will be only for teenagers.
I. Title.
PZ7.T371596Tak   1988   [Fic]   87-23382

ISBN 0-590-41247-7

12 11 10 9 8 7 6 5 4 3 2 1   8 9/8 0 1 2 3/9

Printed in the U.S.A.   12

First Scholastic printing, May 1988

33 511

For all the sources of this stuff,
conspicuously Polly,
with everlasting love and gratitude.

The
Taking
of
MARIASBURG

1

Maria

Maria was shown into the lawyer's office by a gray-haired woman wearing a sailor suit. The lawyer's name was Mr. Byron Godfrey. When Maria walked into his office, he might have been hiding a mouse in his breast pocket, behind the handkerchief.

At last, he did look up at her; he nodded, praised the weather, briefly. Then he pointed at the chair across the desk from him and just said, "Please."

She sat and looked at him, her lips apart and almost smiling, head turned and slightly bent, her eyebrows raised. She was seventeen years old, so who knows how she'd learned to look like that, already.

Mr. Godfrey put both palms flat on the desktop, as if he had to keep the thing from floating up, away from him. A single sheet of paper was between them.

"Congratulations, Maria. . . ," he began, and smiled to go along with that. He said her name like this: Muh-*ree*-a.

"Muh-*rye*-a," the girl corrected him, with a little shake of her head. She had long, wavy brown hair, parted in the middle, and when she shook her head, the hair all swirled and then came back to perfect place again, the way a skirt does when a dancer turns.

"Muh-*rye*-a, then," said Mr. Godfrey, and he looked and found another smile to wear, before continuing. This one was much less dressy, more like yard work.

"You are the luckiest girl in the world," he said.

Maria knew at once what this must mean — what it *did* mean, to him. Somehow, someway, she — Maria — had become extremely rich. Possibly, she now was fabulously wealthy. She nodded at the man, meaning not agreement but: Go on. Tell me about it.

"Under the terms of your late father's will," he said, "you are his only heir. It stipulates that when you reach the age of seventeen and one half years — as you have done, today — you shall receive from me, executor of his estate, a check for all the assets held therein. Less legal fees, of course."

"Of course," Maria murmured. She'd never seen her father, hadn't known if he was late or early or on time. In fact, she'd never heard a thing about him in her life, before. Her mother always said he wasn't any of her business. Her mother was a waitress by the name of Sis.

"It's a very . . . sizable amount," the lawyer said, and licked the pinkish slit he took his meals through. Maria knew he'd like to talk about this . . . fact, however much it was; roll some numbers back and forth. She knew he'd *love* it if she clasped her hands and bounced a time or two. And then ran 'round the desk and gave him one big hug. Asked if she could call him "Uncle Byron," maybe.

Maria stood up and so did he. That way (he figured) he could better catch what he had coming to him. The girl was slightly buck-toothed but emphatically a looker, also stacked. She had a light blue shirt on, with the top two buttons open; he could see the shadowed cleft between her breasts. She was very near as tall as he, and he stood five foot eight. He saw the outlines of her nipples up against the fabric of the shirt, as plain as day. Money turned a lot of women on, he knew. He'd been in that same office all of thirty-seven years, but he didn't think there'd ever been a woman in the place, before, who wasn't wearing a brassiere.

But the girl not only hadn't started moving hugward; she didn't look like she had plans to. Instead, she simply held her hand out — palm up, and the left one.

Mr. Godfrey got the message, went "Harrumph," and bent and flipped the switch that worked his intercom.

"The check, please, Mrs. Farragut," he said. He'd sounded like a game show host. They stood there, him and this Muh-*rye*-a, looking past each other's ears.

"If there should be anything — " the lawyer started up. He cleared his throat a second time. "What I mean to say is, as attorney to your father, I can tell you. . . ," but he stopped again. Maria'd moved her head to look at him, and she was shaking it.

The gray-haired woman came back in, now smiling, this time with a light pink bank check in her hand. She held it out in front, and up a little, the way some wealthy women hold a leash, Maria thought, when there's a little poodle on the end of it. The woman didn't hesitate: she gave the check to Mr. Godfrey. Although the client soon would be much richer than her boss, it was he who kept her in brassieres.

Mr. Godfrey held the check by either end and looked at it, as if it were an ear of corn. Maria hoped he wasn't going to kiss it.

He handed it to her. Mrs. Farragut had stayed, so as to see Maria's face. She could hear herself already, telling all about that moment to her husband. "You should have seen her face. . . ," she'd say.

Maria first checked out the name. They had it spelled right, all in caps, no problem. Then she ran her eyes along the numbers, following the dollar sign. There were quite a few of them, and then a lot of zeroes, before you got to the decimal point — too many to keep track of, really. After the decimal point there was a 7 and a 3. That struck Maria as amusing — seventy-three cents, after all those dollars — so she smiled, and Mrs. Farragut went "Ahhh."

Maria folded the check twice and slid it into the right back pocket of her jeans. All that money didn't even make an outline on the denim, up against her butt; the lawyer checked that out, as she was leaving.

"Well, I guess that's it," Maria said to him. She assumed his legal fees had been historic and proportionate, and she wondered if he'd thank her.

He didn't. The way he saw it, he'd just made a nothing girl a multimillionairess.

After a short wait, Maria turned to Mrs. Farragut.

"See ya," she maintained. And moving gracefully, unhurriedly, she sashayed out the door.

2
Queen of Pizza

Maria decided to deposit the check right away. She had a small checking account already. Her last deposit had been the $50 she had got for being Queen of Pizza.

She took the check and her deposit slip to a teller with a very rigid hairdo. By her window was a black nameplate with the word "Fidelity," in white, on it. Maria didn't know if that was, like, advice, or just her name.

The teller looked at the deposit slip and said, "Hey, good one. Very funny."

She shoved the slip back toward Maria. "I got no time for bull-hockey," she said.

Then she picked up the check and looked at *it*. She saw the name of the bank that it was drawn on and the name of the person who signed it. These were both familiar. She was standing in the first of them; the person was the one she never failed to smile at, every chance she got. Fidelity blinked twice.

"If you will wait one moment, please," she told Maria. She tried to sound a little roguish, like the kind of person who, on second thought, might have a lot of time for bull-hockey. Or other games a customer might think of, and enjoy. Bushmatoozle, cockamautry, weeniewonkers: line 'em up; let's go.

Her hand shot out, as fast and sneaky as a toad's tongue, and fastened onto the deposit slip again. Then, bearing both the check and it, she hustled back to the head teller's desk and handed both of them to him.

Maria saw the two of them confer. He looked up and over at Maria. He consulted the computer on his desk, then snapped a sentence at Fidelity. He rose and sped directly to Maria; she could tell he *loved* the check. He punched out a receipt with careless ease, double-checked the zeroes, and awarded it to her. He called Maria "Miss" and her last name, and pointed out his desk where she could always come for "services" (he tittered), instead of waiting "in a boring line."

Maria fluttered the receipt at him and then, not meanly, at Fidelity, with a little bow and smile. Now it was a fiscal and financial fact: she was a multi-millionairess.

She left the bank. Outside the door she saw a woman who was wearing clogs step directly onto dog-doo. She stopped and offered her a Kleenex.

"Be glad you weren't wearing hiking boots," Maria told the woman, looking on the brighter side of things, the way she now — forever — could afford to do.

Maria decided she'd walk to Seppy's next. She'd tell him first, before her mother. She knew that she could go and buy a car and drive it over, but it was too nice a day to be cooped up in a Mercedes or a BMW, or whatever she decided on. It wasn't until she'd already gone five blocks that she thought of a convertible, and by then she was quite a ways from any dealers.

Another reason for not getting a car quite yet occurred to her: she didn't want to start behaving differently, just because she had a lot of money. You always heard that money changed a person, and if that was so, then probably a lot of money would change a person a lot. And the amount *she* had — taking that theory one step further — might render her unrecognizable.

She imagined herself going into some place like Carmelo High, and starting up a conversation with people she'd grown up with, and they'd go, "Wait. Do I know *you*?"

And she'd say, "Sure. Of course you do. The lake last Saturday. Upside-down canoe racing. The boa, Noah, in the bag of volleyballs."

And they'd go, "But. . . . *Hey!* You *are* Maria! We really didn't recognize you! How is it possible you changed so much — since *yesterday*?"

And she'd say, "Well, I haven't *really* changed, inside. You only *think* I have, 'cause I got rich and all."

Actually, Maria had looked well-off since puberty, or a little after that. Her legs and cheekbones both said this: Big bucks. She might have still been Queen of Pizza on her other assets, though.

It crossed her mind, on the way to Seppy's, that possibly they wouldn't want her to be Queen of Pizza anymore. They might not want, as Queen, a member of the upper crust. Pizza was a kidder, the way the pointed end of it flopped down and dripped. It didn't have a doorman or a dressing gown.

Seppy would like that, though — if they ended her reign and stopped putting her picture in the papers.

"What sort of fool would want his girlfriend to be Queen of Pizza?" he inquired of her, once. "Guys from far away as Mamacita, bones from the Olduvai *Gorge*, for pity's sake, all trying to put their knees beside my squeeze. It isn't worth a few free slices, far as I'm concerned."

It was true. Some pretty foreign groups had come and driven 'round and 'round the block her house was on, some nights, making whoopee sounds. Even her mother hadn't been impressed with that, and she went pretty easy on the sort of noise guys made in groups, which she was apt to call "a little harmless gang-whang-bangling."

Well, Maria thought, the world would still go on if she was Queen or not. But now, when Seppy heard her news, and plans. . . .

3

Fortune-Telling

When Maria got to Seppy's place, she went straight up the drive to what used to be the garage. Nowadays, it was a combination workshop and family room, with benches all along the back and just about every kind of wrench, torch, saw, hammer, screwdriver, drill, chisel, bit, bolt, nut, screw, nail, and empty paper cup that you could think of, as well as a sofa, two recliners, and a home entertainment center. When you opened up the door of the record storage area, you'd find The Boss and Suzanne Vega leaning up against a jug or two of Carlo Rossi. Seppy and his dad were very close.

Parked out in front of this "garage" were Seppy's dad's Corvair, when he was home, and (almost always) Seppy's room, which was on the back of a flatbed truck.

He'd bought the truck when he was fourteen from a small-eyed man in Mamacita named Perry O'Donnell, known (among his brother Elks) as "The Disease." He'd charged the kid 100 hours of personal service and a jar of his mom's piccalilli, which seemed pretty cheap, even for an eighteen-year-old vehicle that didn't run — but O'Donnell would have

10

taken 50 hours, even 25. Fact is, it wasn't odd-or-any-other-kind-of-jobs that Perry O' was after; what he wanted was that relish. He'd gotten a dab of it on his plate at Seppy's mom's church's potluck supper, and as soon as he tasted the stuff, he was sure it was an item. Now it's known as Cephas Sawyer's Original Old-Fashion Piccalilli Sauce, of course, $8.99 the 6 oz. crock, at Bloomingdale's, and O'Donnell doesn't live in Mamacita anymore.

It took Seppy's dad almost a full year to put the truck in A-1 running condition; once he'd done that, and up until the time that Seppy got his license, he'd take it out every few days and run it around town some. By then, Seppy'd finished building his room, too, so people always stopped and looked and pointed at the truck, and sometimes Seppy's dad would stop so they could see the thing up close.

On the outside, Seppy's room looked like a gingerbread cottage in a storybook. It had a sharply pitched tin roof (that gave outstanding rain-sound), but the way he'd done the eaves and painted it, it looked like gingerbread. And on each sloping side of the roof he'd fastened some pieces of white PVC plastic pipe (an elbow on a three-foot length), and painted bright red stripes on them. *Voilà*: two realistic candy canes. The four-paned windows both had tinted glass, and shutters, and the odd-shaped shingles Seppy used for siding looked as if they had a sugar glaze on them.

Both of Seppy's parents were a little surprised when he custom-built his personal space in that particular shape, but they also had to admit that it looked mighty cozy. His mom made red-and-white checkered curtains for the windows before she realized you couldn't see their color that well from the outside, but Seppy liked the curtains fine and hung them anyway.

Maria didn't think that Seppy looked like your average gingerbread cottager, any more than his parents or anybody else did. He looked more as if he'd live in a sleak and narrow, low-slung, mirrored, speed-house, with a lot of sliding glass and gurgle-furniture. He stood six two, every inch of it designed — and some of it developed — in an "interesting" way, Maria thought. He wore a white silk scarf a lot, but never knotted, and he had a lovely, long, lean nose, just very slightly Roman, and shiny, shaggy, collar-length black hair, parted in the middle. Yet for all his fast-lane looks, he was a country road at heart — local, lightly traveled, handy, and direct.

When Maria stuck her head inside the ex-garage, she saw — was glad to see — that Mimimi was there, as well as Seppy. She was blowing up balloons and Seppy was writing words on them in glitter paint. He'd just put ENTROPY on one side of a red one.

"Mya," Mimimi said, smiling. She was Maria's other bosom friend. "Where you been, already? I thought it was that disgust-o time again and you'd gone to get a mouse, for Noah. *He* said more like Fruit Loops, probably. We were arguing. What's a mule skinner, anyway? It don't have scat to do with bedroom slippers, right?"

"No," Maria said. "But stuff all mules and listen up. I want to tell you something major, something that'll change your life. I've come into possession of a *fortune*!"

"Aha!" said Seppy, pointing three-four times at Mimimi. "And wha'd I say? Close counts in horse-shoes, hand grenades, and *guessing*. Are cookies next to cereal at Shop-a-Lot, or what?"

He threw an arm around Maria's neck and held the other hand way up and out in front of him, as if he had her fortune there, in braille, and he was feeling it.

"I see a journey with a handsome teamster — yes, I see a mule, or anyway a jackass. Wait . . . involving a dark stranger, a piano — yes, a baby grand, I think." Seppy took Maria by the shoulders, made her face him.

"Or do you mean a *copy* of *Fortune*?" he asked. "Is it the new one? Lemme see the Corporate Raider of the Month, okay? Has he got big bagonzas?"

"Shut up," Maria said. "I'm serious. I'm just back from the lawyer's and the bank. You can forget money, both of you. My *father*'s left me all the money that the three of us will ever need, and more." She turned to Mimimi. "Or the four of us, counting Roger or whatever his name is, if that works out. My father left me millions and millions of dollars. I'm not kidding. I'm embarrassed to tell you how much."

"Your father?" Mimimi went eyebrows-up at that one. She had a rounded head of reddish curls and very rare and valuable green eyes that looked as if they came from South America, maybe from a river bottom in Brazil. "*I'm* not surprised. I bet that he's been watching over you — forever. Agents of his, and him. He's loved you all along. He couldn't tell you that — he had his reasons — but he did. Didn't I always say?" Her eyes went wide a second time.

"Remember when that fella stopped his car last year? The older guy? When we were walking back from Poncho's? And he asked you — not *us*, but you, specifically — to take a little ride with him? You think that maybe. . . ?"

Maria waved at her, and Mimimi shut up. That fella in the car was not her father; she would have known it if he was. Deep in her heart, she'd always loved her father and known he had good reasons why he *couldn't* show himself to her. But her father was a subject that she wouldn't talk about with Mimimi or Seppy, even. Mimimi would talk about the guy, but not Maria. She always kept her father private, in her heart.

"The thing is," Maria said, "I know already what I'm going to do with some of it — a portion of the money, right? You want to hear?" She grinned. "I think I'm going to have a little town."

4

Buyer's Market

"So, right about the present time, the crowd be-
gins to fret and to *per*-spire. Does — they ask themselves — this soft-spoken, fourth-generation realtor
really know the way to Jacks-'r-better?" No one
said a word, just stared out different windows. Valentino Sandstorm took a breath and went on talking. "Is there still full-bodied faith on unmarked
rural highway number 85? Or does the gauge of
confidence read 'Empty'?"

They'd been doing this for most of four hours:
shifting cheeks on plaid upholstery inside a Datsun
wagon, class of '81. License number: DEALS —
pure vanity. Maria and Seppy were in front, Mimimi and Roger in the back. The driver was the
third word in Sandstorm and Son Realty, Specialists
in Rural Adaptations. He'd shown them two used
towns already, places by the names of Flare and
Crosspatch. Now they were, supposedly, moving
toward another one, this Jacks-'r-better. Not on any
beeline, though. Ever since they'd headed north and
east, away from Crosspatch, there'd been a lot of
slowing down at unmarked crossroads, turning left

one time and right the next, or going straight some more, and sighing.

"Confidence was never in my lunch box," Roger said. "Not on this excursion. Before, at least you looked like you were hoping for the best. Now, I'm betting you're flat lost."

Maria had a lot of reservations, when it came to Roger. His clothes had zippers angled in peculiar places, as if he owned, or possibly had grown, a lot of secret, odd-shaped items. He also fondled Mimimi from time to time, off-handedly, the way you would a lucky charm.

Roger collected professional basketball fights. He didn't like the *game* of basketball, just the not-too-frequent brawls. He'd sit through hour after hour of foul and jump shots, dribbling and dunking, just in hopes there'd be some punches thrown or bodies grappled to the floor, or (all too rarely, sadly) pulling hair and biting. He had hundreds of tapes of these occasions, which had been rated in three categories: originality, belligerence, and humor, with thirty as the top score in each. The ratings had been done by a poll of the members of this association of professional basketball fight fans he belonged to, called "Balltercations," based in Darien, Connecticut. They traded tapes a lot, and sometimes sold them, he'd explained to Mimimi, and she'd said, "Oh, delicious."

"Here comes the truth, now," Sandstorm said. "I'm not what *I'd* call lost. Which is not to say I know *exactly* how to go, from here. Put it this way: we're on the right side of the Rand McNally and we've got it folded like it should be. From here, it's

just a question of. . . ." He took another left. "*Aha!*
Now *this* looks like the highway we've been looking
for." He glanced beside him, at Maria. "*That* left
was right, muh lady."

He'd learned this rule from Sandstorm, Senior:
Always sell the woman. It was important to be *nice*
to everyone, even Min and Biff, the neighbors, who'd
just joined you "for the ride." But it was still *the
woman* that you had to sell.

Maria was that woman here. Valentino had made
sure of that, with her cooperation, long before they'd
even gotten in this car. He wasn't going to take a
joyride with some high school kids for funzies. In
fact, this girl — Maria — she just might turn out to
be The Big One that he'd always dreamed about,
Ol' One Eye, if she'd been a bass. Reel this lunker
in, he'd get a copy of the check for his commission
blown way up and stuffed, hang it right above the
fireplace. He'd never met four kids like these, before. That Roger was a wiseass, senior grade. The
other three seemed nice enough, but not outstand-
ingly brought-up. They had this funny way of
speaking. More or less as if they were the same as
him — like, equals.

Well, for The Big One he could stand it, and he
knew that it was there, potential, provided he could
find the bait: this freaky little ghost town in the
foothills of forget-it.

Mimimi and Seppy'd both looked pretty stunned
when they first heard about Maria's riches and her
town idea.

"A whole *town?*" said Mimimi. "We'd live in it,

you mean? Put down some roots, and that?" She'd fluffed her curls a little. "I think I'd like it if I wasn't just from here."

"Well, that wouldn't be the point, exactly," said Maria. She kept on looking at Seppy out of the corners of her eyes.

"I'm still back on the money," he said. "I haven't even gotten to the town part, yet. You really are that rich?"

"Yes," she said. She pushed up the corners of her mouth with her two forefingers. "That's good, don't you think?"

"I don't know a lot about it," Seppy said. "On TV, the guy who wins the lottery always says he's going to be the same. And then you see him in a white suit, smoking a cigar."

"With a bunch of girls," said Mimimi. "A lot of times, the guy is sitting down and about five girls with tits out to here are leaning over so's their heads are all around the guy's, like he's a daisy. They're in the chorus, where he's staying."

"Yeah," Seppy said. "They're all rubbing his bald spot, for good luck."

"In the *pictures* it's his bald spot." Mimimi rolled eyes.

"You *guys*," Maria said. "*I'm* not getting in the papers. This is something different, something personal."

Seppy laid his paintbrush down. He'd just put FLESHPOTS on a blue balloon.

"I know," he told Maria. "It just takes getting used to. The same as if you cut your hair all off — please don't, it was just an example. It'd still be you."

"But why . . . how come a *town*?" said Mimimi. "Specifically. I can't remember any time you said you wanted one, before. *Earrings* I remember, sure, but not a town."

"No," Maria said. "I never did. But when I got this money — well, what happened was, the *scale* of everything got changed. You know? Like when you learn to drive, and time and distance get all different? Before, there wasn't any point in wanting something like a town, but now there is. And so I thought of it."

"But still," said Seppy. "Why? Other than the fact you could afford it."

"*If* we had a town" — Maria said it slowly, softly, emphasizing every word — "we'd get to have some time that wasn't any of their business."

"Time," said Mimimi. "It's time you're really after, then. The town is just a space to put the time in."

Maria nodded, solemnly.

"And *they*? The 'they' in 'their'. . . ?"

"*You* know," Maria said. "All the ones with scorecards. Everybody that I have to please, or else. Gimme a break. Start with Sis and just go on from there."

Seppy held up a finger. "All the people who consider themselves to be in a position to do you political, economic, or sexual favors?" he asked. "Members of the clergy, the medical profession, and police?"

Maria smiled.

"And closer to home, we have every member of the instructional, athletic, and guidance departments at Carmelo High," said Mimimi.

"Absolutely," said Maria.

"Not forgetting Mrs. Considine at work," said Mimimi, "and the Admissions Committee at the University of Everywhere."

"Which leaves," said Seppy, "more or less just — "

"*Us*," said Mimimi, "and any other persons almost totally lacking in power and influence. They'll need a town like that forever."

"Welcome to Mariasburg," said Seppy. "Population: 18 — and under."

Jacks-'r-better was a wholly different thing than Flare or Crosspatch. We're talking Packard, maybe, as compared to Henry J or Edsel.

Flare hardly rated as a town at all; "Call it, like, a real bad guess," said Valentino Sandstorm, later. Any route you came, you saw it baking from a lot of miles away, a place where narrow, black-topped highways crossed. On one corner was a scavenged Sinclair service station and garage with a couple of pipes sticking up out of the ground in front of it, and a stanchion with the old round Dino sign, now pocked with bullet holes. Diagonally across from it there was a weathered, gray dilapidation, having four sag-steps up to a rotted porch, behind which was an empty opening as wide as five Rotarians. Tacked above it was a square tin sign. "Drink Salada Tea," it said.

Sandstorm stopped the car and everyone got out and read the beverage instruction. Maria shook her head and got back in the car.

"Beam us out of here," she told the realtor.

"Here's what I have to say concerning Flare,"

said Roger. "Someone ought to set a couple out before you get to it."

Crosspatch at least had a few trees around the four surviving structures. It also had a present population, lying in a hammock. His slick-over hair was about the color of the dusty pickup parked beside him, and he told them he had plans to turn the town into "a Mecca for gambling." He said he had to send for a "per*mit*," he guessed. When he got it, he was going to change the name of the town to Croesus. That was more of an upbeat, optimistic name, he said. Among other things, he was worried about "Crosspatch" attracting a lot of sore losers. Roger looked around at all the square miles of empty land surrounding Croesus and told the guy he thought he'd be all right for parking.

Jacks-'r-better was up on higher elevations and was much more of a place than the other two. Mimimi decided it had character. For one thing, it was built on both sides of the road, and probably was twenty buildings strong.

Valentino Sandstorm pulled right in beside the biggest one, a church, and they got out again. The steps up to the doorway of the church were hardly worn at all. There was one of those letter-boards at the bottom of the steps with this leftover message on it: "ALL REPUBLICANS AND DEMOCRATS ARE DOPES AND DUMMIES."

"Well, here she is," said Sandstorm, looking up this main street at the other buildings. "And take my word for it: You're not going to find a town for sale in this kind of a shape or condition but, oh, *once* perhaps, in any span of fifty or a hundred years. I know *we've* never listed one this nice, and

21

I include my father and his dad, before me."

Maria found she could relate to that. In terms of trash and blight and pure bad taste, this empty town looked better than a lot of places with a Board of Health, and self-appointed consciences, and zoning.

"How come?" she said. "How come it's stayed so nice?"

"First," he said, "we've got the fact you're off the beaten path up here. Way off of it. No one lives for miles and miles around — you saw that, coming up. Then, too, a fella with a Buick Special and some romance on his mind, he's got so many places on the way to here that's every bit as nice and private, that long before he makes that turn back there, he pulls it off the road and says to her, 'Hey, *hell* with it. Come *on*.'"

Roger nodded absentmindedly at that and got his palm on Mimimi's rear end.

"It also helps," said Sandstorm, "that there's only one way in and out of here, and this is private property belonging at this time to Hupee County. People over there would dearly love to see it on the tax rolls once again, at max evaluation, if you take my meaning. So if the sheriff ever chanced to find some trespassers or vandals up this way, believe me he would throw the book at them. Targeting the places it don't show too much, like over and around the kidneys."

Seppy looked away and started whistling.

"Finally, you've got your real dry air plus altitude," the realtor continued. "A town is like a person, when it comes to aging. Nature plays a part and so does nurture, am I right? Places have good genes or bad, the same as you or me. Maybe now that we are here with my veracity intact" — he shot a glance at Roger — "you'd like to hear some local history."

"Roll 'em," said Maria.

"The town of Jacks-'r-better," Sandstorm said, "was founded by its builders in the early eighteen eighties: the lumberjacks who cut the first-growth timber here, the giant sapwood trees you only see in photographs these days. This was a race of *men*: independent, hardy, not the kind that liked to live by other people's rules and judgments. Apparently, a gang of them was working in this valley and they fell in love with it — quite understandably, correct? — and bought the whole dang shooting match, some five–six hundred acres, from their bosses. Once the trees had been done in and floated out of here as logwood, the barons had no use for it, rapacious as they was." He nodded firmly, twice, on that one: Sandstorm, spokesman for the common man.

"Jacks-'r-better was the name they gave the place — meaning, *lumber*jacks of course, themselves. Most folks think of poker, but not so. In any case, these better 'jacks, they built a solid, sturdy town — you'll see that when you see the sills and beams they made — expecting their descendants would hang onto it forever." Sandstorm sighed, then bent his head and pursed his lips and let a foamy blob of spit drop out of them and darken up the dust.

"Of course that didn't happen," he went on, "human nature being what it is. Their kids despised the place. Being kids yourselves, you'll maybe see their point, in one respect. If Jacks-'r-better isn't any-

23

where today, imagine where it was in nineteen nine. Six years after that, the last of them, the founders of the town, gave up and said to hell with it. They sold it all — the houses, land, and right-of-way — and moved to San Magoo."

"In nineteen — what? — fifteen?" said Mimimi. "That was during World War I." She snarled at Roger, faked a gouge-out at his eyes, her first two fingers spread to make a fork. He turned his head defensively and took his hand back off her ass.

"Correct," said Valentino Sandstorm. "That war was why there was a buyer, you could say: the Sisters of Sanity. Now, contrary to what the average person might think, the Sisters were a lay association, not religious in the slightest. What these ladies were was basic radical extremists, feminist persuasion, separation-minded. Politics, they said, makes people crazy and wars are started every time by crazy politicians, men who thought that everybody else should look at things the same way *they* did. So, the Sisters said, to hell with them. They weren't going to be a part of any craziness. They moved up here to Jacks-'r-better and declared the town completely party-free, and separate from all patriarchal rules and regulations. It wasn't that they didn't like the men, it was the politics, hy-pocrisy, and wars they couldn't stand. Any man who swore to give up politics — and looking down his nose at them — could come on up and have a nice ham dinner, with pudding for dessert.

"Well, apparently," (said Sandstorm) "not a lot of men bought into that — it's possible they didn't like the sound of 'party-free' — and once the war was over, they had trouble getting any convert *women*

24

up here, either. Oh, a few did come, when World War II began — they ran an ad in *House and Garden*, I believe — but after nineteen forty-six the population just wore down and finally out, last year. The county took it over for the taxes. But as I said before, it's still got lots of miles in it. The 'jacks and Sisters, *they* wore out before the town did. A little paint, a pane of glass or two, you're right back into showroom shape again."

Maria checked that one with Seppy, and he shrugged and nodded. She then looked up and down the road that they were standing on: Highway number one four eight in Hupee County, Main Street of the town of Jacks-'r-better. Past this close-to-mint-condition church, there was an open space and then a dozen different buildings, side by side and touching. These had a common wooden sidewalk, like the ones you see in western movies, built up off the ground and looking solid. Beyond these buildings were two other separate houses. Seppy could imagine bearded guys in red-and-black checked shirts, with double-bitted axes leaning up against the buildings, sitting out on massive wooden benches, playing checkers. The buildings all were different heights and shapes, with different roof lines. The 'jacks liked living close to one another, Seppy thought, but also made it clear they had their tastes. The houses all looked square and sturdy, though; as Valentino Sandstorm said, those places had some *wood* in them.

"So where's the nearest mini-mall from here?" asked Mimimi. "The place a girl'd go to get some mules skinned, or the like."

"She means the *hub* of Hupee County," Roger

said. "The seething center of intellectual and artistic ferment. Where possibly a friend of hers — not her, you understand — could find a little X, and like — *you* know — some different color watch straps."

"The nearest *town* of any size is Hupee City," Sandstorm said. "The county seat of Hupee County. A pretty town, a prideful town, a town that keeps its picket fences white. We're talking 'magnet' when we mention Hupee City; we're talking can-do, all-America, and *now*. Growing at a button-busting pace, my friends. *Super* place to raise a family, from what I understand."

"Wait," Maria said. "I must have blinked or something. *We* saw all that, coming over here?"

Sandstorm smiled and shook his head.

"Oh, no, indeed," he said. "Hupsie's over that-away." He pointed straight across the street, where the rest of Jacks-'r-better's houses were, with the river right behind them, followed by a range of hills.

"*We* drove north and east, you follow me?" he said. "And the City's more or less northeast from *here*. As the eagle soars, perhaps ten miles away. Take the roads, we're talking more like thirty-five."

Maria looked at Seppy. "Now you ask him stuff," she said. "I don't know the questions guys would ask. Sis kept that kind of stuff from me, the rat. But I know we ought to throw a lot of tough ones out. And get a lot of real right answers, or we walk. That's the way it works, I think. We'd wait until he takes us back to town, though, before we do the walking part."

So Seppy made believe he was his father, and trotted out a bunch of dandies — about the deed to the land and title insurance, and taxes and the water supply, and whether there was any asbestos or formaldehyde in the buildings, and who was responsible for the maintenance of the road, and were there any rules concerning mobile homes that looked like gingerbread. Stuff like that, and more.

After every one of Sandstorm's answers, Seppy nodded. He also graded them as "Good," or "Fine," or "Excellent," and at the end he told Maria: "Sounds like everything's okay."

There was a pause and then Roger checked to be sure about the electric lines they saw connected to the buildings and to find out whether there'd been any talk about cable up there.

After that there was a longer pause, and then Maria said, "I'll take it."

5

Gaps

It was during Sis's afternoon break the next day that Maria dropped the news on her. There was no more devastation than a water bomb would cause; they didn't even need a slicker for the fallout. That was the way things went in their relationship. Different as they were, they were identical in one respect: they loved each other terminally.

Sis worked both shifts at Grantham's Quality Restaurant. Lunch was 10 to 2, a lot of double charbroiled Mexican on business talk croissants. Dinner was the same in terms of hours, being 5 to 9, but dinner was the main event, the big one. Sis always came home for a couple of hours after lunch to grab a shower, change her uniform, recharge her batteries, and memorize the dinner specials; she'd do the last part in front of a mirror, checking out her posture, timing, smiles — the total presentation. Sis was always sky-high going into dinner, psyched.

When she had something personal to say, discuss, Maria liked to bring it up at 4 P.M. That'd give them forty-five full minutes, aka enough already. Maria told Sis once she didn't have to be there for a particular conversation if she had something else she had to do — that she could read both parts, if need be. But Sis said no to that one; she *was* a mother, she explained, and she had her job to do. No matter what, she said, you didn't give your kid free turns. Maria said she'd known that she was going to say all that.

Because of the demands of Sis's profession — vocation, really — Maria did most of the cooking at home, but on this particular afternoon, in a burst of mother-feeling, Sis had made them both a cup of tea, and even asked Maria if she'd like a half a Danish. Maria took the tea, but turned the pastry down. She didn't eat that kind of junk, and also didn't want to have to suck her fingers, while admitting millionaire-ness.

When she did, at 4:02, telling Sis both where the money came from and the fact that it was "millions" (number left unspecified), Sis only shrugged and said, "That's typical. I'm not surprised."

Maria didn't know whether her mother was referring to her father's dying or his leaving her the money, or both. But *she* wasn't surprised, either. Her father was one subject Sis would change, as soon as it came up. She loved to talk about Maria's clothes or horoscope or hair or boyfriends, or all about her getting Queen of Pizza, but this heiress topic came and went in fifteen seconds flat.

Not so with item two, however, the news Maria'd bought a town. That was an issue, an event — and a mistake. Sis found her place at once.

"A town?" she said. "A *town*? Oh, *honestly*, Maria. You've gone and bought a town? You *dip*! That's totally ridiculous. What on earth does a seventeen-year-old girl need with a town — *another* town be-

29

sides the one she lives in? Oh, no. I can't see that at all. I really can't."

To be sure of that, Sis squeezed her eyes completely shut and made her pretty turned-up nose go back and forth a while. She fished a Salem out, by feel, from the soft pack on the table, right in front of her. A customer of hers — this medical supplies salesman — had told her how he'd heard the menthol that they had in Salems was the exact same kind they put in the astronauts' lozenges, to suck in outer space. "You don't know what a sore throat is," he'd said, "until you've tried one *weightless*."

Sis lighted the cigarette with a disposable lighter that said "Ernie's Plumbing and Heating" on the side. She'd opened up her eyes, and she was looking good; she heard that twenty–thirty times a normal working day, and it was true. She had an unlined, youthful face; her hair, though waved and set, looked soft and touchable. She'd kept her trim shape, too; she was a graceful straight-line stepper, with a saucy little sway. Sis was thirty-six, not counting.

"Try again," Maria said. "How about a town as an investment? Leave out bagel shops in West Beirut, and real estate is close to fool-proof. You buy some real estate and keep it for a while, and then you sell it at some gross humungous profit. Take your mother on a trip around the world."

Sandstorm had mentioned the investment angle more than once, and so Maria didn't hesitate to bring it up. She liked it when she used a smokescreen made of real true smoke.

Sis shook her head again. "It isn't all that simple," she explained. Maria knew what she'd hear next: the women-always-take-a-screwing bit.

"You always make things sound so simple," Sis went on. "But they aren't. You want to know what happens when you buy a town? I'm speaking of a *woman* now, like you or me. I'll tell you *just* what happens. No sooner do you buy yourself a town than you are right up to your rosy-red in fifty different things you're not cut out to deal with. Take my word for it; *I* know. All this shit comes flying down, you wake up bleeding in a ditch some place."

"What?" Maria said. She had to laugh. "A ditch? I'm going to buy a town, not some old Harley Davidson. You're being crazy, Sister. Paranoid. As usual."

"Am I?" Sis inquired, and she laughed, herself. "You think I'm being paranoid? Well, supposing I just give you *proof*, Miss Tootsie-Town? Ms. Roll-Your-Own-Metropolis? A prime example of *exactly* what I said."

"Lay it on me," said Maria.

"Geraldine Ferraro," Sis said calmly, and she nodded once, for emphasis. "Right? What did I tell you? *Sister picked a piece of perfect proof,*" she chanted. "A child of five could see it. Tell me she don't *rue* the day she ever started up with all of that. A customer of mine — I'm pretty sure he was a lawyer — told me just the other day. He wouldn't be surprised she's in and out of courts another twenty years. When they get through with her, she'll be lucky if she's got a pot to piss her Pepsi in. And why? Because she tried to do a thing she wasn't suited for. Wasn't *made* for, if you want to know the truth."

Sis laughed. She gave herself that round, round one. She was having fun. They had the best relationship she'd ever heard of a mother and a daughter having. Neither one of them was out to change the other one, not any way at all.

Sis put down the cigarette in one of her souvenir ashtrays. She'd been collecting them since high school and now had over two hundred, "every one in working condition" as she'd tell a customer, sometimes. This particular one, she'd gotten on the Cully Island Indian Reservation. It was shaped like a tepee. You put the cigarette inside it, and the smoke'd come out the top, real cute. Maria had grown up with ashtrays everywhere, all over the house — three, for instance, on the toilet tank. She'd never smoked, herself.

Now Maria had to answer Geraldine Ferraro, move the argument along.

"Nowadays," Maria said, "women own all sorts of property. Ranches, mines, even some pool halls, Mom. Men have gotten used to that, believe it. Put politics aside, we're talking real estate. Suppose there's only daughters in a family. Who do *you* imagine gets the real estate, when both the parents kick? You think it's going to go to Bill the Cat, or someone?"

"*You* know what I think," said Sis, with nothing else in mind, for the moment. If Maria wanted a town, let her have a town. Hell, it was her money. But it was only half past four.

"It's not a question of nowadays, or any other time," she said. "Although as a matter of actual fact, from everything you read in the papers there's more *peculiar* and unnatural acts being performed every day, nowadays, than any time since . . . whachamacallit" — she took a chance and said it fast — "Solomon Begorrah." Maria bit the insides of her mouth and Sis continued.

"This has nothing to do with a person's age, intelligence, or what the neighbor's letting *her* kids do. What I'm telling you — everything I say — is based on *feelings* that I have. Never mind statistics and all that. *Feelings* happens to be the one thing a woman knows more about than anyone. And the one thing she can *trust* when all else fails." She stopped and looked Maria squarely in the eye.

"Right?" she asked. "You *know* I'm right on that one."

There it was, Maria thought. The Everywoman-Has-Her-Feelings argument — a tough one to completely contradict.

Maria did her usual, a sort of nod-shrug-nod. The trouble was, she did, in fact, believe that she, and other women she had known including Mimimi at times — and maybe guys as well, like Seppy was a candidate — *did* have access to some knowledge (truth) they'd never studied (learned) from anybody else. Things that *came* to them, and which were much more *right* than other things that "people said," for instance.

Maria called the feelings that she had "pure" feelings. They were the ones a person was born with, that were there *before* you started learning what you ought to think and do, according to your parents, teachers, politicians — the authorities.

It was nothing against Sis, but Maria noticed that a lot of what Sis thought were *her* feelings had been made in someone else's factory. Every time Maria heard "Do unto others before they have a chance to do unto you," or "If anything can go wrong, it will," or "God has a special thing for America," or "Nice girls don't," something deep inside of her would just go: *Clunk. That can't be right.* She didn't make an issue of those things; she simply didn't believe them. By the time Sis noticed, she figured that it didn't matter. She loved Maria as she was, the way that she'd "turned out."

One place that Sis's feelings and Maria's didn't match at all was on the matter of women's roles. Sis felt that women were put on earth to take orders from men. All sorts of orders, actually, but beginning with: "Let's see. I guess I'll have the pot roast, mashed potatoes, salad. . . ." This belief had "come to her" when she was seventeen. It had happened in the banquet room of the Holiday Inn in Mamacita. She'd been taken on as a temp for the Rotary luncheon, and as she brought those men the fruit cup or the soup, whichever one they wanted, and they started eating it, she'd gotten this feeling of contentment ("rightness, you could say") she'd never had before in her entire life. From precisely then — that moment on (she always said) — she *had to be* a waitress.

Maria's explanation of the same events was different. She figured that the Rotary guys had smiled at Sis, and tipped her, maybe spoken highly of her fanny; afterwards, the manager had offered her a full-time job. None of those nice things had ever happened at Sis's parents' house, where she'd been treated none too well in general, from what Maria'd heard. Waitressing had got Sis into an apartment of her own and, in time, a husband and a baby girl (Maria guessed).

34

But now Maria had to use the Everywoman-Has-Her-Feelings argument herself, in her behalf.

"But that's my point," she said to Sis. "My *feelings* are what tell me I should buy a town and live in it a while." She made her most sincere persuasive face. "My deepest, truest female feelings."

"Are you completely sure of that?" asked Sis. She smiled and aimed another weapon, a real heat-seeking missile. "I'm your mother, so I read you like a book." She'd convinced herself that reading Maria like a book was a feeling, too, though it was actually one of the things *her* mother had said that she'd sworn she'd *never* say to a child of her own.

"You don't *want* to settle down and get married," Sis continued. "You don't *want* to get yourself revved up for college — although God knows you could waltz right into the University, and a lot of others, too, as slick and easy as an eel on ice. Which I'm sure I needn't add would make your mother — who never had an opportunity like that, she was so busy being a *mother*" — Sis overdid a sigh — "*deliriously* proud and happy.

"But you *do* want Mother off your back," continued Sis. "Or, as you would say, 'to live your own life for a while.' Which as far as I can see means doing absolutely nothing normal. That's why you *really* want this town of yours."

And Sis sat back and smiled, as if she'd cured the common cold.

"That's cute," Maria told her mother. "Now your daughter is peculiar and perverted. This is the thanks I get for twelve years on the Honor Roll, membership and even offices in clubs and teams, a social life untainted by disease or scandal — plus being monarch of the house of mozzarella. Given that record, for you to predict that I'll do 'absolutely nothing normal' in the future is not — oh, no — not just unfair, illogical and . . . pukey. It is also, clearly, slanderous. And so, my dear, you are disqualified. The court has ruled a mistrial, and you are liable for damages. Not only are you out of time" — Maria tapped her watch — "but also you are out of guesses, spins, predictions, and opinions. Pay the bailiff as you leave the room. I thank you."

Sis looked at her and smiled some more. Maria was her father's child, no doubt about it. Her mind ran on like his did — wonderfully, but not a cinch to understand. Probably, she thought, Maria should have been a boy. Perhaps she *was* a boy, except for parts and plumbing. Sis figured that was possible. It'd be sort of like having a Buick engine inside a Lincoln Continental body. The car'd look the way a Lincoln Continental did, even when you got inside it, but it'd work just like a Buick.

"All right," said Sis, "all right, all right, all right. I didn't think you'd pay that close attention. I probably shouldn't have said you weren't normal. You're normal enough, I guess." She phony-sighed again. "What you are is *unrealistic*, more than any other thing." She stood up. "Anyway. I've got to run. Prime ribs tonight. You know what that means." And she kissed Maria on her part, scooped up her cigarettes and lighter, grabbed a lightweight jacket, and was out the door.

Left behind, Maria made a face. "Unrealistic," was she? Nonsense. What she really was was *anti*-realistic, and proud of it. Realists, it seemed to her, were people who believed in present day "realities." The realists she'd known were smug and plausible. If you disagreed with them, it wasn't *them* you disagreed with (so they said), it was the existing "facts."

"I'm only being realistic," they would smirk.

The way Maria saw it, reality was often in the eye of the beholder. Many times, it happened that "realities" were simply things that people *hoped* were so, or *said* were so, at least. Example: We're in danger of attack by Nicaragua.

Or take for example the "realistic expectations" that the principal (and other power people) at Carmelo High had for all the students there. They, those students, were expected to:

1. Learn at least 70 percent of the "material," whether it was of the slightest interest or use to them, or not.
2. Work at "jobs" which would teach them the value of a dollar — while putting a minimal number of same in their pockets — and which would also help them to find out what they might want to do for the entire rest of their lives, career-wise. Not *not*-want, *want*.
3. Experience "healthy relationships," or possibly "love" or, if not either of those, at least find out how a lot of stuff works — "stuff" being male and female anatomical parts and various ways of exciting or controlling them.

If people failed to do #1, above, they were, "realistically speaking," not college material. And if they hadn't done #s 2 and 3, tough, because it was now

37

up to them to make a few fairly major decisions having to do with production, *re*production, acquisition, housing, matrimony, et cetera. Of course they weren't too *practiced* in making major decisions like these because, during high school, they weren't *mature* enough ("speaking realistically," of course) to make *any* of the important decisions about their attendance, programs, attitudes, teachers, materials, and so forth. Those decisions were all made *for* them by people employed by the school who therefore, supposedly, had a real good grip on the "realities" of life. You could tell that by their personalities and value systems and, at times, their politics. Sure, you *bet* you could.

People like Maria, though, who were "realistic" degree candidates at college, could have four *more* years of 1 and 2 and 3, four *extra* years to learn about themselves and that big world out there, before they'd have to bounce the first against the second. The smarter you were, apparently, the *more* time you were given to learn to cope with the realities. That made a lot of sense, Maria thought. Sure, you *bet* it did.

But no matter which group you were part of, you were told (and not just by high school authorities but by city, state, and federal officials right up to the tippy-top) that you were absolutely opportunity-*engulfed*, that you could "have it all," if only you'd just "go for it." If anyone felt anxious, fearful, rushed, confused, or undefined, well, realistically, that was *their* problem. The system couldn't do it all; there're always going to be a few failures.

Maria reached into her shirt pocket and took out the folded check that she'd made out that very morning. She slid it under the edge of her teacup. It had been a first class cup of tea, but Sis would still be thrilled to get a tip like this one. Half a million realistic dollars, and she hadn't even had to split the Danish.

6

Speaking of Mariasburg

"When I think of it," said Mimimi, "like first thing in the morning, I get this Christmas feeling in my breath-box." She touched herself below the topmost buttoned button on her open-collared blouse. "Or it's the morning of the day you're going to get your braces off."

"Me, too," Maria said. She took a bread stick. The two of them were playing Ladies. By some computer error, both of them had double lunch on Tuesdays, and they'd gone to Mamacita to disport themselves at Pharaoh's, starting with a Perrier, of course. ("I'd like a stalk with mine," Maria'd told the waiter. "No, not a twist, a *stalk*.") Ladies always ate a rotten diet lunch.

Mimimi let fingers float across the table, flutter down on Mya's bread stick.

"Should you?" she inquired.

"I'm only going to toy with it," Maria said.

"Of course," said Mimimi, and took her hand away.

"It's funny," said Maria. "But it's not the money, I don't think. That's not what's giving me the feeling. It's like this rush of freedom, not-to-worry space, almost. I guess the money's *bought* that, though."

"It's what you said before," said Mimimi. "The *time*. I've thought about that lots. In all my life — the part that I remember, anyway — I've never had a single day. Just totally for me. A day that I controlled from start to finish."

"A day when youyouyou could totally express yourself," Maria said, and smiled.

"Um," said Mimimi. "And now I'm looking at a bunch of them, lined up for weeks on end." She shook her head. "I won't say that it doesn't have a scary side. What if I blow it? Life calls my bluff." She fingered an imaginary mustache, twirled the end of it. "Okay, kid," — in a big, deep voice — "now show me who you really are." She shook her head again and stirred the bright green celery around her Perrier. It fizzed all right, but subtly.

"It *is* a sort of second coming," said Maria. "Although the first one hardly counts, except as a prerequisite. Just think what happened that time, right away: there you were, a helpless, brand-new baby girl, and some big doctor yanked you up by your feet and swatted you a good one. Talk about symbolic. And prophetic, right? Then pretty soon after that you get to be a kid, with *homework*, and all this other bullshit starts coming down that you've just sort of got to *grope* your way through and build up defenses against, and all — oh, thank you," she said to the waiter.

He'd put down a large pink plate in front of her. A fresh apricot half on a thin smear of yogurt looked like a fried egg. ("What fun!" Maria pointed at it, sticking up her thumb.) There were also four green beans criss-crossed like in tic-tac-toe, with the spaces in between filled either by black ripe olive slices (making o's), or x's out of pure white pasta, neither one victorious. A tiny Boston lettuce leaf supported a single chicken nugget, sculpted in the shape of a frog.

"A person *needs* a second coming," said Maria, "to properly appreciate a lunch like this."

"What it does, I don't mean lunch," said Mimimi, "is give you time to take just about everything you've been given as a goal or value back to the customer service desk. And tell them you've decided on a whole new wardrobe."

"Of course it's possible you'll just go naked for a while," Maria said. "And then make up your own stuff, piece by piece and bit by bit, out of all this real pure silk you've got inside you."

Mimimi laughed happily at that. "I like it," she agreed. "Two sassy silkworms on our way to being butterflies. And we can change our names to Eve, all right? Though this time let's make lemonade and *sell* it to the snakes."

"Maybe just until you get your outfit ready, we better leave old Roger off at Crosspatch — I mean Croesus," said Maria. She cut a bit of green bean with her knife and ate it. "Not that he couldn't handle you without your Calvins on." She laughed.

"Oh, Roger's not so bad," said Mimimi. "A lot of what he does is just for show. But speaking of . . . *you* know. Well, I've been wondering about that part. Up there." She smiled. "What *about* my father's favorite subjects: sex and drugs and Does-he-drink-like-beer-or-what-?" She spelled out OXFAM on her plate, cutting up the beans to make the F-A-M. Then she popped the whole piece of chicken in her mouth and started chewing it.

"Oh," Maria said. "I thought we'd ask them for a froggy bag." She looked at Mimimi's plate, and then she pushed a green bean through her olive slices, imagining them as black plastic bracelets on a long green wrist.

"You know," she added. "I don't think I like being Ladies any more. Maybe it's because I can afford it. Isn't that peculiar? It's like I'm really one of them, and so. . . ."

"You ought to be a good example," interrupted Mimimi. "But as a matter of policy I refuse to listen to any of your vast-personal-fortune guilt trips. And I didn't hear an answer to my orgy question. I can guess what you and Sep and me — and even Roger if he comes — would do up there, how *we'd* act and all. But, like, who else is going to come? Assuming other people want to, and you want some different campers. You're not just going to post a notice on a wall somewhere — or are you? Like a sign-up sheet?"

"No," Maria said. "No — yikes — that could be disastrous. I thought I'd maybe ask some people, though. I know that sounds . . . elitist, or something. But they wouldn't be some special group of chosen ones — just people who we thought might really want what we want. Need it even, maybe. And who'd also be a little cool and keep their mouths shut." She looked around until she caught their waiter's eye, and then she lip-synched: *Check?*, counting on his memory to hear the word off earlier recordings.

She looked at Mimimi. "Does that sound awful? Asking people?"

"I don't think so," Mimimi opined. "At least at first, for starting up. But who, for instance?" She was curious. Maria was a person everybody liked or — put it this way — who no one didn't like. She wasn't part of any group at all. Guys didn't altogether *get* her, because although she wasn't shy, or distant, she didn't *date*, exactly. She hung around with Seppy quite a lot, but she didn't behave like his girlfriend; mostly, she was just one of a whole bunch of people. Girls were puzzled by the way she sat with different individuals at lunch, including some endangered species. Mimimi and Seppy were the only two at school who knew that she was straight and that the President had made her cry. But not when he was tugging at the nation's heartstrings, talking heroes, or feeling real emotional himself; it was other times, his ways of acting "peaceful."

"Well, possibly The Guise," Maria said.

Mimimi just had to gape at that, her green eyes huge as swamps. Depending on the person that you talked to at Carmelo High, The Guise were either (simply) "music," and the greatest, or a total off-the-wall type mess. The band had started out as being four hard rockers, boys of course, and then it got . . . experimental. Now, it numbered twelve, four of whom were female. Two guitars, a bass, a contrabassoon, keyboards, congas, drums, a flute, a tenor sax, and three vocalists, one of whom would sometimes swing a mean green tambourine. A dozen reputations, also, one per person.

"Wo!" said Mimimi. And then, reflecting, "Neat-o. Anybody else?"

44

The check arrived on a little flowered plate. Maria looked at it and made a face.

"This is really sick," she said. She got some money from her shoulder bag and set it down on the saucer with the check. She was imagining all the seeds or powdered milk or oral rehydration stuff the dollars lying there could buy. She imagined this piled up on one of Pharaoh's big pink plates, a great serious heap of necessary food, now spilling over the edge of the plate, covering the whole table, dripping down onto the floor.

"Who else?" asked Mimimi, again.

They stood up. Maria started naming names; she sounded angry. The names were mostly geeks and nature children, bad girls, absentees. No one from the center of the stream: fringe-o's, wonderers.

"Maybe some of them," Maria said. "I guess we'll see." She switched her eyes to Mimimi's. "It isn't you I'm mad at."

"Okay," said Mimimi. What she cared about was being just with kids who chose to be exactly where they were, for once. And who (therefore) laughed a lot and hoped for things beside a lot of *things*.

"I almost just can't wait," she told Maria.

That night Seppy and Maria drove his room out to the mall and picked up a half-price pizza to go, which they then brought back to his driveway and ate in his room in their underpants. Maria had a cami on, as well, a white cotton one with a little lace on top. She always sprinkled red pepper flakes on her part of the pizza and they made her sweat. Particularly her head, but her legs, too, she said, if

45

she really got going on the pepper flakes.

The real reason she was eating in her underpants, though, was that she didn't want to drip tomato sauce on her clean white duck trousers. She asked Seppy if he'd take off his jeans so that she wouldn't feel . . . peculiar. He wasn't hard to get along with. His underpants were black and hers were blue with thin white stripes. Neither pair made much of a dent in the world's cloth supply.

When they were through eating the pizza, they started trying to throw their wadded-up used paper napkins into one another's open mouths. Maria always claimed she opened twice as wide as Seppy did, but it was still a pretty even game they had. Mouth-ball was more something intimate to do than a win-lose situation, and they both got really pleased, whenever one popped in.

"Sep?" Maria said. This session of the game was getting old.

"Yuh-huh?" he answered.

"Are you okay about the town?" She was on the bed and propped up on his pillow, feet curled back beneath her bottom.

"I really am," he said. "As far as I'm concerned, Mariasburg is homemade apple pie, straight from the oven. It's beautiful up there. We're going to feel like people in a storybook. Like. . . ." He raised both hands and moved his head around as if to say: The same as we do here.

"But by the way," he also said. "When, exactly, were you thinking of. . . ?"

She said, "I really hadn't. Any time would be all right with me. Tonight" — she smiled — "the first of May. It really doesn't matter."

"Well," he said, "it seems to me that we'd be crazy not to wait till after graduation. Why make extra trouble for ourselves, is what I say."

"Trouble?" said Maria. "How?" She switched her legs around, stretched them straight on down the bed, and leaning, touched her pointed toes.

"*You* know," he said, looking not at her but out the window, at his parents' house.

"Is it snowing out?" Maria said.

He moved his eyes to her and saw the little waiting, smiling look — the one she'd also thrown at Mr. Byron Godfrey, the attorney.

Seppy rubbed his knees and laughed.

"No, it isn't snowing, and you *do* know what I mean. A lot of people — jerks I grant you — are going to think our doing this at all is crazy."

"Is it crazy?" asked Maria. It was always possible that having — getting — all that money had unhinged her, she supposed. "Eccentric" was the word that *went* with "millionaire." So far, she hadn't had an urge to saddle pigs or show up at cotillions with a rope and ice ax, wearing crampons and a gear sling, but she reckoned it *could* happen.

"No," he said, "of course it isn't. But if I was a college admissions guy, I might think it was. Or, say, a person doing interviews for jobs. The first thing that some dude like that might think — supposing that he sees this in your bio — is: Hey, this kid went off and started up a *commune*. Which, of course, to him equates with either dope or standing on your shaven head and chanting ooga-boogas. Right away he'd have some . . . questions, but more so if he saw you didn't finish high school with your class. That you dropped out in the middle of the

47

year to just go off and vegetate. According to *him*, that'd be — the 'vegetate' part."

"Uh-huh," Maria said. She moved her fanny on the bed again, this time over near the wall so she could spread her legs apart, almost in a split (but keep them on the bed), and do some sideways stretches, twisting, leaning over first one knee and then the other. "What kind of questions do you guess he'd have, in general?"

"Oh, probably he'd want to know what sorts of kids were up there, what they *did* all day — maybe what the *rules* were. In your case, whether you were just endowing other people's weirdness, you might say." Seppy rubbed his jaw. Maria thought he looked like someone in a Bic commercial — not a tennis player.

"Sepper?" said Maria.

"Hum?" he said.

"Now that you've had time — a few days, anyway — to think about this scheme, do you find you're feeling . . . *trapped*, at all?" She was sitting in that same position with her legs still wide apart, and now she leaned way forward, resting on her elbows. She had her eyebrows up again, and she was also smiling, but she didn't cock her head.

Seppy rose and went and sat down on the bed beside her pointed toe, the right one. He dropped his left hand on her calf and squeezed it.

"Trapped?" he said. "No way. This boy is *striding* toward his destiny — whatever it may be — unfettered and unchained. He's clear of eye and firm of jaw and . . . and moist of palm, of course."

He reached and took Maria by the shoulder, and she swung her legs together so's to give him room to stretch out there beside her on the bed.

"Although his heart is pounding rapidly," continued Seppy, "with pulse to match, he's not remotely influenced by any personal considerations, such as those of any gland-involving nature, your psycho-sexuo-romantico component, if you take my meaning. I mean, if I were *trapped*, there'd have to be some *bait* somewhere, and how could anyone believe" — his hands were spread out on Maria's back, underneath her cami — "that shoulder blades like *these*, and *gluteii*" — he changed his grip somewhat — "if that's the plural of this section. . . ."

"Seppy," said Maria, her lips right near his ear.

"Yo," he answered.

"Just shut up," she said. "All right?"

"Clang," he said, and kissed her.

7

Ups and Downs

It was sort of depressing to realize that even with all the money in the world it'd be semi-dumb to bug out of Carmelo High in the middle of the year without a piece of paper — a diploma, a *credential* — from the foolish little thing. But once she'd thought the matter through, Maria had to see — and then to say — that Seppy had a point. As well as other ways to get around (et cetera) a girl. She liked the latter far, far better than the former, but it was that college argument of his that got her to the Guidance Office and a date with Mrs. Winslow.

"Well, Ma-*ree*-a," Mrs. Winslow said, "according to the information in your folder here, you've got your applications out to Watson, Brink, and Eastman, as well as to our University. Is that correct?"

"My name's pronounced Ma-*rye*-a," said Maria, "and — "

She stopped. Mrs. Winslow had her hand up like a traffic cop and was looking through Maria's folder, doing little head-shakes as she turned the pages.

"No," she finally said, "we don't have any record

of Ma-*rye*-a. Is that something . . . rather *recent?*"
And she smiled.

Like the light blue orchid tattooed on my der-
rière? Maria thought, but didn't say. Instead she
matched the lady's smile and only said, "No, it was
my mom's idea. The day I was born, I guess."

Mrs. Winslow made a note, right across the folder's front: "Pronounced Mah-righ-ah." The same
note in the same handwriting, but tinier, was written on the folder's tab.

"Well, that's all right," she said. "So let's get back
to work, here. Now, let's see. You've got your applications out to. . . ."

Maria let her run that line by one more time. And
when she heard ". . . correct?" she said, "The reason that I'm here is that I've decided not to go to
college in the fall. I was wondering about my op-
tions. About deferred admissions, in a nutshell."

"What?" said Mrs. Winslow. She drew her brows
together and started leafing through the folder once
again, a good bit faster, this time. "Not to go to
any college in the fall? But Muh-*ree*-a — no, Mah-
righ-ah, sorry — I don't think you want to do a
thing like *that*. That wouldn't be a good decision
for a girl in your position. With your *scores*, I mean.
And Mr. Peterman has given you what I would call
a *glowing*. . . ."

Maria waited patiently. She'd folded her two
hands, demurely crossed her ankles. She'd even borrowed Sis's circle pin and pearls, that morning. She
certainly did not chew gum, and for all Mrs. Winslow could tell she had both bra *and* bloomers on.
When a song ran through her mind, while Mrs.
Winslow was talking, she made sure that it was

one — like, "Lonesome Town" — which Frank Sinatra had recorded.

But in spite of all these preparations and precautions it took her almost forty minutes to get Mrs. Winslow to accept as a possibility that she was *not* going to go to college in the fall, and that her mother "allowed" her to make her own decisions concerning her educational future. She also found out how deferred admissions worked, and that there was no way she could have back any of the various essays that each of her colleges had made her write, as a part of the application process. Even if she wasn't applying for next fall and might have wholly different answers in another year or so.

(Here are some examples of the grist Maria had to grind, for one place or another: "If you had to choose one color to describe yourself, which would it be, and why?" "To what extent have the events in the Near East and Central America affected your idealism or your cynicism, or both, since junior high?" "Describe the most admirable, *or* the most despicable, man you've ever known, or known about, other than your father or President Reagan." "What skills, qualities, or connections do you possess that would be apt to thrill, inspire, or enrich your fellow students here?")

"Thank you very much. You've been a big, big, help," she said to Mrs. Winslow, standing in the doorway of the Guidance Office, just in case those words provoked a lightning strike.

Mrs. Winslow knew she should look up and smile, herself, but talking to Maria had depressed her. For weeks thereafter, every time that poor girl or her namby-pamby mother came to mind, she couldn't help but start to shake her head. *That Muh-ree-a,* she kept saying to herself.

It seemed to Maria, during the next weeks (which added up to months, in time) that she'd gotten back on board the Life Express: the silly train of circumstance that carried everyone through high school to their Future, rocketing along and never pausing to take stock of what was really going on. This leg of the journey seemed to her to be a particularly absurd one, for on it she was going to have a "senior slump," apparently — a thing the teachers both expected and resented, but felt powerless to counter. *Why don't they send me to Mariasburg?* Maria wondered. But of course she knew the answer. One, they didn't know that it existed. And two, this way, although she might be wasting time, at least that was the way it (always) was, and therefore proper. *Realistically,* it happened. Hell, a lot of teachers there had gone through the senior slump themselves, and look at them, how they'd turned out (they told themselves).

But although no one sent her there, Maria made it to Mariasburg four times, when it was springtime. Twice, she drove herself, with Mimimi, in Sis's Honda. Otherwise, she went with Seppy, the first time in his room, the next time in his dad's Omega.

Maria took a lot of photos every trip, so she could dazzle Sis — and also any kids she'd later talk to — with just how beautiful it was up there. The more she saw the town, the brook that flowed beside it, and the woods surrounding everything, the more she fell in love with all of them.

The brook was clean and fast, more like a small

river, really, and Maria remembered it had been used to float the timber down, a hundred years before. She could imagine the 'jacks dancing on the logs, jabbing at them with those pointed poles they had, and falling in sometimes, and hollering. The river, it was drinking-fountain cold. The woods were warmer, great to walk around in — not a lot of heavy underbrush and brambles; Maria guessed the trees in it were "second growth," feeling like Miss Forestry when she thought that, but they were getting pretty huge, a lot of them. She'd also seen some deer tracks by the water's edge.

Seppy, after leisurely examinations, said the buildings in the town were every bit as good as he'd first thought. In all, there were exactly eighteen houses, ten of them divided into two or more apartments. There were also storefronts, eight of those, and one large structure Maria assumed was a hotel; it had a room downstairs that still had tables and a bar in it. Seppy said perhaps the Sisters of Sanity had used the place for craziness, on weekends.

The first spring trip Maria took was one with Mimimi. They got there Friday night. The breeze was warm and soft, and the leaves were rustling. Maria felt aglow with freedom, with a kind of basic decency and gentleness. She said just that to Mimimi who smiled and nodded, touched her cheek. All Saturday, the two of them explored, in and out of every building in the town from top to bottom, deciding which ones they'd have dibbies on. Two just fantastic places that they found were in the belfry of the church, no more than halfway up the tower and below the pointed spire that it had. Maria said she wouldn't be surprised if the 'jacks had built the church so they could make a steeple, too; the thing was that impressive, just a slender, soaring, wooden work of art.

But right below it were these spaces she and Mimimi adopted for their own. Up a little winding staircase was the first of them, a cozy, square-shaped room with windows all around, the room they'd used to use to pull the bell-rope from. And in its ceiling was a trapdoor (and, of course, the rope-hole), going up to where the bell itself had hung, when there had been a bell; they guessed it had been sold to help pay taxes at some point. The views from there were almost scarily magnificent, seeing that there weren't any walls to speak of, just a guardrail and the four huge corner posts on which the spire rested. Maria loved it way up there — in the crow's nest, as she thought of it — the more so when she realized that she could pull the ladder through the trapdoor after her, and shut the thing, and bingo!: total privacy. So she'd laid claim to it, and Mimimi (who was, in fact, not all that fond of heights) agreed to "settle" for the room below it. "I *guess* I'll let you have a right-of-way," she told Maria, grinning.

Sunday morning, while Mimimi still slept, Maria wandered down and took an icy dip, before she'd had her breakfast, even. She walked back up the slope to the town, wearing just a towel around her neck and feeling like Sheena, Queen of the Jungle. She dried off in the sun, sitting on the wooden sidewalk, looking down the Main Street of the deadest, dearest town she'd ever seen.

* * *

55

Mimimi came out and found her there and gave her quite a scolding. "All these years, and not a breath of scandal, and now *this*," she said. "Get inside, you shameless hussy. . . ."

Maria flicked the towel at her, stood up and strolled — on purpose, with a hip-switch — in the opposite direction from her clothes. She had business at the church; she'd just remembered.

Not inside the church, although it did occur to her that it was Sunday and maybe she should preach a homily on . . . Joy . . . and Talents (say), to all those empty pews. She'd seen a theater in the round, why not a sermon in the nude? Of course she wouldn't do a thing like that, for all she'd like to, in a way. The spirits of the 'jacks might possibly misunderstand and think that she was mocking them, their church — whatever. Mockery was not Maria's style. It was the lingua franca of Carmelo High.

No, what she had in mind to work on was the message board outside the church, where it said:

ALL REPUBLICANS AND DEMOCRATS
ARE DOPES AND DUMMIES

She didn't think that was exactly true — and anyway, there should be changes in the message, every now and then.

The problem was, she was limited to just the letters on the board. Maybe there were more somewhere, but they hadn't found them on their exploration.

She scratched her head, and after several false starts, came up with this:

56

She put the letters that she hadn't used in a neat row, underneath.

Then she walked back to the house they'd spent the night in, stuck out her tongue at Mimimi — now soaking up the sun herself, but primly in her rolled-up shorts and t-shirt — and went inside to dress.

When, two weeks later, Seppy saw Maria's message on the board, he asked about the change. He'd parked his room beyond it, in the church's parking lot.

"You mean what that things says?" He pointed at it, smiling.

"I don't know," she said. She'd pinned her hair up and was wearing his Giants baseball cap, but backwards, and his Forty-Niners jersey, Joe Montana's number. "I can see it either way, depending on my mood, I guess." She hadn't talked to anyone about that subject, except for Mimimi, a little. When Mimimi had seen the sign she'd just said, "Fuck 'em. I agree."

"Oh, yeah?" he said.

"Well, sure," she said. "Just think. You put in any rule that maybe someone wants to break sometime, and you've got . . . trouble. Any time you have a rule, you've got to have a penalty. Or else *what*? And penalties — they stink."

"But if you don't have any rules," he said, "you can't protect yourself from . . . well, the biggest asshole on the reservation."

Maria nodded. "The rotten apple in the barrel.

The slither-guy inside the garden." She sighed. "It's real depressing."

"What?" he said.

"The awesome power of evil." He made a sound. "Don't laugh," she said. "Think how quickly I can make you feel like shit, even if you're in a real good mood beforehand."

"True," said Seppy, and he pulled his nose. They were just sitting there in the cab of his room. "And the flip side is: There's no way I can *make* you happy, if you're sad."

"Absolutely," said Maria, nodding. "Although I think I know some girls who *totally* believe they'd be in heaven, if you tried." She grimaced, and then smiled. "Of course, with me" — she slipped a hand around his neck, a little finger in his ear — "you do have ways to make me happy-*er*. . . ." She laughed.

That night, Maria fell asleep with all her clothes on, there on Seppy's bed, lying in his arms, her back against his front. Later on, she had a dream of being at a stock car race, surrounded by a lot of people who she didn't recognize at all. She and Seppy were sitting on the back steps of his room, watching the races, and all around them were these guys with beards and woolen watch caps, knocking back a bunch of beers and hitting on some girls with not that great complexions, who were wearing tight black jeans (white stitching) and these ribboned peasant blouses.

"Put the pedal to the metal," different ones kept hollering toward the track. From time to time, they'd look over at the gingerbread house (and her and Seppy), and snicker something back and forth. Finally, this huge fat guy wearing bib overalls and a green bandana around his neck and black boots jerked his thumb in their direction and said, "Or put the leather to a little fairy tail or two," and everybody laughed.

The next morning, Maria found fresh tire tracks outside the church, right there in front of it — the kind those heavy-treaded tires make, the ones that go to ATVs of different sorts.

And there was also a different message on the board outside the church. It said:

DON CUM BAC U SATAN PEDERMASTERS

The other unused letters were just scattered on the ground.

8

Ins and Outs

When Seppy and Maria'd looked, and seen that message on the board outside the church, they'd made a face. Not the same one; different faces.

"This town's been ravished," said Maria.

"Hold on," said Seppy. "Maybe 'pedermaster' is meant to be a compliment."

"Very funny," said Maria. Remembering her dream, she wondered if perhaps it hadn't been a sleep experience at all. Weirdos looking in their window while they slept. Disgusting and . . . embarrassing. It wasn't, but it could have been. Maria liked her privacy.

"The thing *I* wonder. . . ," Seppy'd said. "Let's take a ride, you want to? Seems to me I've read about. . . . Forget it. Just come on."

They'd gotten in the truck and wheeled on down the highway, slightly grim around the gills.

As soon as they'd got home, on Sunday afternoon, they went to Mimimi's and told her.

"There's like a little *cult*," Maria said. "We went and talked to different people and found out. They

60

live out on a farm. No one else within a hog call and a half. What?" She turned to Seppy. "Ten miles from the 'burg?"

"More like twenty-five and cult is *her* word," he told Mimimi. "We're talking maybe seven stick-soids, here. Oddball Armageddonites."

"They think the rest of us are toast," Maria said. "Or will be, on the day. Burned in hell, of course. And they *also* are believed to put their kids in cages. *And* to have a ton of military stuff, enough to overthrow the government of . . . I don't know, like, *Utah*."

"I guess some people think that they've been stealing stuff," said Seppy. "Livestock, mostly. But some tractors, too. That and other farm machinery."

"Tractors, *wow*," said Mimimi. "A hot *tractor* ring, in our own neighborhood."

"It isn't funny," said Maria. She picked up one of Mimimi's father's famous chocolate-chocolate-chip cookies, a big fat one. "These creeps were in our *town*, we think. There's one called Sledge. He's meant to be the leader."

"Sledge — that's gross," said Mimimi. "Like *sludge*, but harder-hitting." Maria gave her a look.

"What the sheriff said when we went to Hupee City," Seppy said, "is anyone can drive through town. Mariasburg, I mean. The county owns the road, it's public access. But stuff like what they did is trespassing."

"The sheriff's quite good-looking," said Maria. "He said he'n the boys'd keep an eye out. That's just what he said: 'Me'n the boys'll keep an eye out.' "

"*How* good-looking, one to ten?" asked Mimimi.

"I'd say an eight point six, six, six," Maria said.

"Point six, six, six, sex, sex," said Seppy. "One of those repeating decimals in real tight double-knits, cream-colored Stetson hat to match. I'll tell you, Mee. This guy's to Roger as . . . oh, maybe John Travolta is to Cheech or Chong."

"Gee," said Mimimi. "*That* close."

"But anyway," Maria said. "We spent last night there, too. Right in the parking lot beside the church, *again. He* went straight to sleep, of course." She pushed on Seppy's shoulder. "And did his famous length-of-giant-redwood imitation, all night long."

"Miss Delicate, Miss *Vigilant*, never closed her eyes, however," Seppy said. "According to herself, that is."

"And no one came in town at all. On foot, on horseback, or riding in a four-by-four," Maria said. "We aren't going to let the bastards spook us, that's what we decided. If we've got The Guise and a bunch of other kids up there, it's The Defenders of the Fate that better watch it."

"That's what they're called? The Defenders of the Fate?" said Mimimi. She cupped her hands, as if she held a crystal ball in them. "The Fate of the Defenders? Yes. I see them shackled in a hot manure spreader. The sheriff — looking like Don Johnson in this episode — now starts it up and drives *his* tractor, an *extremely* streamlined cool one, up and down this great big field. Little bits of pure fanatic fly out everywhere. And next year they get more whatever — weeds, I guess — from that one field than any time in all recorded history."

"Yucky-poo," Maria said. But it was nice to have such fearless friends, she also thought.

"*Hey*, Guise," said Maria. She was standing right beside the E-Man's tom-tom, two feet from the mattress-covered wall in Boid's garage. Boid played tenor sax. In legal fact, the garage belonged to his grandparents, both of whom were very near sublimely deaf. *They* played a card game by the name of booray. Neither of them drove, not anymore.

"Hey, Mya," "Hi, Maria," "Scooby-dooby-doo," "Wha's happening?" said different members of The Guise. They were into heavy sweating, having just stopped playing/singing/beating out a song, "How High the Moon." It has a line in it that goes: "Somewhere there's music — how faint the tune." Not in Boid's garage, though.

"Look," she said, "I know you're busy but I want to tell you something. E said he'd give me two whole minutes. Thanks, E-Man." She smiled at him. "That should be plenty." She took a real deep breath. "So here it is. You won't believe this, maybe, but it's true. I've got a little ghost town in the mountains, and I'm going to live in it a while. Starting in July, or maybe sooner. You guys could live there, too, if you wanted to. It's going to be a place to live and work on stuff without a lot of outside pressure. Free room and board. No frills." She smiled. "Just me and Mimimi and Seppy and some other kids. Everyone'd pitch in on chores, like meals and maintenance. And . . . oh, yeah — we'd leave our stashes, anyone that has one, somewhere else." She said that fast and dropped her eyes, then raised them. They were all still there. "I guess that's it. Here's some

pictures of the place. I can come back if you're
interested. Answer questions, stuff like that. Do me
just one favor. Maybe it's impossible, but . . . don't
talk about this with a lot of people. It's just . . .
you know. It's not the place for everyone."

Maria thought her voice seemed really small and
wimpy, hushed by all the insulation in the place:
old mattresses and carpets, that pink panther stuff.

The Guise looked both at her and one another.
Everybody knew Maria. She was not a jiver or a
joker. What she'd just offered — said — was, like,
their wildest dreams come true. In other words,
impossible.

"You're serious," said Parmenter. He played the
flute, a long, lean black guy with a little sea-straw
cap on. "You're *serious*, Maria." It was not a question, but it was.

"I am if you are," said Maria. "Don't come if
you're not serious. I'll check it out with E next week.
Till then, I'll see you all. Well, 'bye." And she was
out the door.

"Later, M-word," said the E-Man, just as stunned
as anyone.

"I really think I'd like to," Willa said. She and
Maria were sitting at a table in the school cafeteria,
and Willa was holding one of the most delicious-
looking sandwich-halves Maria'd ever seen. It was
all she could do to keep herself from snatching it
out of Willa's hand and stuffing about half of it into
her own mouth. It — and it had been the one in the
baggie Willa'd opened up at least ten minutes before — was made with *obviously* homemade bread
and seemed to contain Swiss cheese, sliced toma-

toes, sprouts, and maybe turkey; a drop of Russian dressing had dripped out of it, since Willa had been holding it that way.

"I have to force myself to eat, sometimes," Willa said. "But it's getting much, much easier. And also I've stopped throwing up." She looked down at the sandwich in her hand, smiled at it, and then (*at last*, Maria thought) she took a bite, a small one.

Willa was a tiny, skinny girl who cut school very frequently and didn't make much of a dent in the days she did show up. To most kids, and a lot of teachers, she didn't seem to be quite worth the effort. Maria, effortlessly as always, had found out that she was not just sweet but also very talented and medium messed-up. But working on the last part.

"Everyone is going to do some kitchen work, I guess," Maria said. "But I was thinking, if we had a person who could order food and plan the meals and maybe supervise the cooking, some of it. . . . There'd be a stipend, of course — don't I sound efficient? What you've got to understand, though," she went on, "is you don't *have to* do that. It was just a thing I thought of, 'cause you cook so great. The whole point of the place is everyone can be themselves. Do mostly stuff they really want to do, or think they'd like to try. The Guise, for instance — they won't want to work on space designs, like Seppy plans to do. And if I had to eat the stuff they seem to go for. . . ."

She'd gone back to Boid's garage three days before, by invitation. It was Saturday, the band was on their lunch break, junkin' up. Turned out they wanted *in*, ecstatically, though certain of their parents still posed problems. Before, they'd planned on getting part-time jobs and playing gigs a night or two a week, or as available. Mariasburg (as E-Man said) was like a patron saint, a sponsor and deliverer. Not to mention a rehearsal hall. Of course they'd daily and *most cheerfully* contribute labor to the common weal, he said (the band all chorusing agreement). And even volunteer to "foreswear all illegal changes of their consciousness while physically in residence."

"Plenty-fella say we won't get high up there," said Sophie, as translator for Maria, self-appointed. Sophie was a vocalist/arranger. She had styled and frosted hair resembling a wave about to break on her left shoulder. Maria thought it looked half-past sensational.

Willa was thrilled to hear The Guise would be in residence, as well. She said she'd love to be the chef up at Mariasburg. Opening an inn or restaurant someday was on her list of hopes or possibilities.

"The Anorexic Arms," she told Maria. "Can't you just see it? Little pipestem of a place?"

Maria laughed. Giving time away was proving to be easy, just about a snap.

9

Population Problems

They decided that June 28 would be Opening Day. At first, Maria'd thought it'd be fun to make a wagon train, a caravan: line 'em up, roll 'em out, excitement sparklin' the frosty morning air (regardless of the temp, outside), wagons stretched as far as eyes (or youse) could see.

Seppy said why not just take an ad in all the local papers, or hire a sound truck. He'd put his hands around his mouth to make a megaphone. "Grand Opening Today!" he called. "A Town for Teens in search of Time! Music! Girls! No Realistic Rules! Free room and board! Directions on request."

Hearing that, Maria made a face. Seppy had no romance in his soul. Seppy was a practical pig. And maybe worst of all, he probably was right. She held her own hand just below her mouth, as if she had a microphone in it.

"There's been a change of plans, *vaqueros*," she intoned. "Everybody take a different trail than everybody else. Make absolutely sure you aren't being followed, even by de dog. Hour in between each wagon. No one blows their horns, including all you cattle. And stow that gingerbread affair inside a prairie schooner, Sundance."

Mimimi and Willa both rode up with her. They left at 3 A.M. Seppy was going to start a little later, using his room to haul a ton of food. Roger, who owned an '82 Camaro, said he'd leave whenever he woke up, probably about eleven.

"It must take him half an hour to zip up," Maria said, on hearing that.

"You're *bad*," said Mimimi, but she was laughing, too.

The population of the town, to start with, would be twenty-six. Maria thought that was a nice, companionable number. Not so large as to become impersonal, but still enough to make a fringe group think a time or two before attacking.

For a while, she thought the number might be larger, but there were parents, quite a few of them, whose first reaction to the town was what Maria called the "clutch" reflex ("their children to their bosoms," understood). They liked what it would cost them: nothing; it was all the rest that they objected to.

Maria went and talked with some of them, like Gina's parents. Gina's parents said there ought to be some adults at the town.

"But why?" Maria said. "Specifically."

"For *guidance*," Gina's mother told her.

"What we're trying to do," Maria said, "is take responsibility ourselves." *Responsibility* (she knew) was not a buzzword but its opposite; responsibility was *chimes*.

"We hope to learn to make intelligent decisions

the same way that our parents did, learning by experience," she added, widening her eyes for . . . emphasis. "Isn't that the best way, really? That's what *my* mom says."

"Um," said Gina's mother, looking at her husband.

"The other thing," he said, "is if you had adults up there, they'd see to it that certain things don't happen." He nodded at his wife and she returned the nod, pleased with his plain-speaking.

Maria'd ridden down this road before. It ended at a thick brick wall, and her without an air bag. She made her eyes get even wider. "Like what?" she said.

"*You* know," said Gina's father, looking at the carpet.

"Don't try playing dumb with us, Maria," Gina's mother said. "You know exactly what he means. This isn't personal, you know. No one's saying it's the sort of thing that you yourself would get involved in. Probably you wouldn't. But try and tell us that it isn't going to happen at a place like that."

"Look," Maria said. "Let's be a little *realistic* here, all right? What's happening this minute, here in town? A lot of kids *are* having sex. *And* getting drunk and throwing up on lawns and doing drugs and getting mangled in a car wreck. If adults could stop those things from happening, they would. But the fact of the matter is, they can't. Not here, not there. Only kids can stop it — that's the truth." She felt like giving them the bird, for emphasis, like Lily Tomlin might have, but she didn't.

"Be that as it may," said Gina's mother, "I know something else that's true: When the cat's away, the mice will play. You take those hippie communes in the sixties; we saw what went on then, without adults around. We weren't always middle-aged, Maria. We were kids ourselves, you know, once upon a time." Gina's mother blushed, as if embarrassed by this past of hers.

"If your mother wants to let you go up there, that's up to her, but Gina's staying home," she said.

"That's inconsistent," said Maria, thinking what the hell, why not. "Two years ago, when Gina's sister Martha graduated, she got *married* in July. She left home and went to live with just *one* other kid and started making all her own decisions, just like that. I don't think they rented an adult to tell them what to do or not to do." She made a robot's voice. "Stay off the chandelier, you kids." Gina's dad looked puzzled. "Why does Gina have to be protected, any more than Martha? And how about if Gina were a boy? Hey, I bet you'd let a Gino go, all right." Maria smiled, the red flag right between her teeth.

"Number one," said Gina's dad, "she's not a boy." He looked a little pissed, admitting that. "And if she was, the chances are she wouldn't even *want* to go, you know? And number two — like Martha's case — marriage is a different deal than going off somewhere with thirty other kids. Getting married shows you're ready for responsibility. Marriage is a part of *life*."

"And anyway," said Gina's mother. "Gina *isn't* getting married. She doesn't even have a steady. Gina's staying home and working down at Penney's. When she's old enough to make her own decisions, she'll see we're right on this."

"End of conversation and case closed," said Gina's father, getting up and heading for the kitchen.

Inviting The Guise had been a great idea, Maria felt. They provided numbers and an attitude. In addition to the twelve band members, there were six "intentional others" (as the E-Man called them) who were hot to come along. E-Man told Maria they had "expertise in areas of sound, et cetera, you dig?" Maria said she did. Turned out she'd met all six, one time or another. All of them were dropouts, two of them were guys. All of them had pretty lousy job-jobs, in spite of having grade A look-looks.

The other three recruits, not counting Willa, were driving up together. They were Jake, the driver, who liked to draw and paint and hang around with Seppy talking shapes/perspective/space, and a king-sized, awkward nature boy who everyone called Babe (the Great Blue Ox), and a girl with frizzy hair named Sookie. She, like the other two, was in their class at school — also in the arcades in the daytime and the bars at night. "You really are a scream," she'd told Maria, once.

Maria'd seen her on a park bench, eating chips and watching children playing hopscotch, and she'd gone and sat beside her on a whim. She'd told her what Mariasburg was all about and asked her what she thought.

"What I think of such a place, like, as a — whachacallit? — *concept*? Or would I want to go?" said Sookie.

"Either. Both," Maria said.

71

"It seems real nice. I can't imagine what I'd do up there," she said.

"Hang out. Turn pages. Act extremely cool. Figure out a game plan. Get in shape." Maria shrugged. "That's what I intend to do."

"That sounds a little slower than the breakdown lane," said Sookie. "That sounds more like the *shoulder*."

"Yeah," Maria said, and smiled at her. "Name a better headrest, though. Frankly, I can use a break. Some time to just collect myself."

"What *I* could use," said Sookie, "is a first-class, one-way ticket right the hell away from here. Maybe to Hawaii." She thought that over, chewing on a thumbnail. "That's what I say, anyway. But you know what?"

"No, what?" Maria said.

"Chances are that I'd be just the same no matter where I was. Face it, I'm not what you'd call *cut out* for doing anything. I'd rather fuck around. Win the lottery someday." She laughed.

"Well, no harm asking," said Maria. "If you change your mind, just let me know." She started to get up.

"One thing," said Sookie. She put a hand out on Maria's elbow. "You asked about *me* going to this place. Does that mean anybody can?"

"No," Maria said. "It's not that big, and anyway, a lot of people wouldn't want to. I'm asking certain ones, is all."

"Like who?" the girl persisted.

"I don't know," Maria said. She didn't like to use the other names as bait. "People who don't seem to know what's next. Like me. It's no big deal. Just real exclusive." And she smiled again.

"You really are a scream, you know that?" Sookie said.

Three days later, Sookie came up beside her in the hall, at school.

"Do you mind if I ask you something?" she said.

"I won't know until you do," Maria said.

"Okay," she said. She took a piece of paper out of her shoulder bag and read off the names of eight people in their class and the one behind it. "Just tell me yes or no. Would you ask them to go up to your place? Any one of them? Or have you?"

"No," Maria said. "I wouldn't and I haven't." The eight included boys and girls, affluent and poor, fireworks and bozos. Maria knew them all. What they had in common was that they were world-class sons of bitches, all of them.

"Thanks," was all that Sookie said.

But two days after *that*, Maria found her sitting on the steps outside her house, the first thing in the morning, smoking a cigarette and reading her and Sis's morning paper.

"Hey," Maria said. "Come in and we'll play house. You can have a cup, a glass, a plate, a bowl. Whatever you can stand. My mother's still asleep."

"I've been out walking," Sookie said. She looked more like she'd been rolled over, slapped around: smudges on her cheekbones and her lipstick smeared and swelling in one corner. "I've. . . ." She started crying. "I've thought it over and I want to come to your place, to the town," is what she said, although it took her quite a while to get it out, in bursts, with sobs between.

Maria put her arms around her. Sookie smelled like one real sad saloon, giving off a warm, thin atmosphere of perfume, body odor, beer, and cigarette smoke, nothing real original.

"Sure," Maria said. "No problem."

10

Communing with Each Other

The Guise's attitude was obvious as soon as it or they pulled into town. They'd driven up in six not-real-new vehicles, one of them a panel truck that bulged with sound stuff, mostly. Another two were vans with homemade paint jobs.

They'd asked, before they came, if they could live together, the dozen in the band, plus six ("their better half," as they described themselves, sometimes). That meant they'd have to stay at the hotel, or whatever it had been, the largest building in the town, the one with the main dining room and kitchen. No one else objected to that plan, so what The Guise did, as soon as they'd unloaded, was to set up on the hotel porch and jam for joy, beginning with a wildly futuristic "Avalon." ("A tonal tribute — a magnificat, a paean to our totally mellifluous surroundings," as the E-Man later put it.)

Meanwhile, Willa, with help from Babe and Jake and Mimimi and Sookie, got the kitchen organized and put a meal together, while Seppy and Maria, joined by Roger when he got there, did some distribution work and housekeeping: putting soap and light bulbs in their proper places, starting the hot water heaters, pumping up some air mattresses — different things like that. By the time the population settled down to eat, the sun had set and it was murky-dark outside, but in the dining room the mood was Day-Glo orange. So what if no one knew if this would really work or not? So what if seven Ma's and Pa's had said this was a "trial," not a commitment? So what if one of them — Maria — had to keep on saying to herself: "You're not responsible for anybody else's happiness"? The meal was plain delicious.

"What, exactly, is the drill here, babies? Is everybody meant to love each other? Or do we get a choice, like, take a number?"

That was Roger's initial contribution to the first night's meeting, once they'd finished dinner. He wasn't a Carmelo kid, so other people didn't know if he was serious. Maria semi-wished that Roger had another zipper, halfway up his face.

Mostly, though, the people rode the meeting cautiously, feeling pretty much the way beginners on a skateboard would. Take the matter of meals, for instance. Breakfast, they agreed, would be an everybody-gets-his-own, starting almost any time. And sandwich-makings, fruit and soup and salad would be out from 12 to 2, each day. But when they got to talking dinner, Seppy jumped right up. And then blushed at that big boldness.

"Look," he said, "I plan to take a lot from people, here." He smiled. "Ideas and food and rides, and entertainment."

"And probably some ex-cre-ment, from time to time," said his pal Jake.

"For sure," said Seppy, trying out another smile and seeming slightly shaken for a moment (thought Maria). He looked down, took a breath, and then continued, speaking quickly.

"And I guess that other people probably will do the same," he said. "I mean, get help from different friends of theirs. But what that is is mostly one-on-one, you know? It's personal, you could say selfish, in a way. So what I'd like to say — suggest — is that we all do certain things for *everybody* else. That there be stuff that everyone agrees to do. I was thinking about dinner as one of those things." He pinched his lower lip. "What I'm proposing is, I guess, that all of us agree to have a *dinner time*, each night. Any time is fine with me. But I'd like to make that kind of a *commitment*, you could call it, to everybody here. To say that you can count on me, for that and other things that maybe we'd agree on." He paused again. "Hell, this isn't coming out right. Do you see what I mean? Am I making any sense to anybody else?" He sat down quickly.

"You're talking, like, a social contract, man," said Parmenter, the flutist. "Where what we do is say that this-and-that are things we all agree to do, to make the whole deal better."

It was then that Roger chose to fire off his awkward little questions. Some people laughed, but awkwardly. Then, silence.

Maria rose and said, "When I first daydreamed this, I had it be a lot like home. People living on their own and doing their own things. But having one main place to cook and eat made sense. And when Willa said she'd like to run it, better yet. What Seppy said is like a whole new *concept*, Sookie, right?" The girl looked startled, then looked up at her and smiled, and nodded.

"I like it, but it makes me nervous," said Maria, going on. She looked at Seppy. "Being more of a community, I mean. But if other people want to have a common dinner time at night, that's great with me. Then we could sort of wait and see."

The room broke out in nods and murmurings, people looking here and there to check the mood in general.

Mimimi got up and said, "Well, while we're at it, there are some . . . *commitments* did you call them, Sep? Such a nicer word than *jobs*. Commitments that we need to have to make our little world go 'round and not grow mold. If you don't believe me, you can ask my mother, without whose help this list could never have been so complete. . . ."

She went on to mention kitchen work and bathroom duties, trash collection and disposal, other functions in and on the different buildings there. Nothing all that fun.

"If those assembled have the stomach for it," Mimimi went on, "I can fix it so that Ace here," she jerked a thumb toward Roger, "feeds this work and our identities into his portable PC and lets it mix and match a schedule." She let her head go left and right around the room. "I'd ask for volunteers for all the jobs instead, but no one looks that dumb."

Again, the noises of agreement came, and Mimimi sat down.

Boid, the tenor man, got up.

"I'm curious," he said. "Here we all are. I've counted twenty-five or six. I know what everyone connected with the band is going to do — and Willa, here. But how about the rest of you? Would you mind saying? And one other thing. If I put up a net for volleyball, and marked out a court, would other people want to play? Like, maybe after dinner, sometimes?"

"After *cleaning-up*, you mean, I'm sure," said Roger, brattishly, and Sophie leaned toward E-Man, whispered: "Just who *is* he, anyway?"

Judging by the group's reaction, volleyball was everybody's favorite game. Boid's other question might have seemed a little *probing* for just then; a lot of people passed. Seppy and Jake didn't mind saying they had plans to remodel most of the apartments in the side-by-side buildings across the street from the hotel. They called their work "interior design" — then had to laugh, self-consciously. Jake also said he was going to paint a lot, and set up his ham radio equipment somewhere. There weren't any phone lines up there, yet. Babe wanted to have a garden and a woodpile, too. He mentioned both of them, as projects, but not the five empty notebooks in his knapsack, or his headful of ideas, some of them for poems.

In general, the women kept the lower profiles, though Mimimi declared that she was thinking of forming "The Anti-Abulia Society," and had tentatively scheduled its first meeting for the next day, after lunch.

"What's abulia?" Maria queried, promptly.

"It's sort of like a phobia," said Mimimi. "An abnormal inability to act, or make decisions."

"Oh," Maria said.

"So," said Mimimi, "you coming to the meeting?"

"Gee," Maria said, "I'm not sure. I *may* go, possibly. But also, I may not. I'll just have to think it over. It seems like it might be a good *idea*, but I'm not sure if I — "

"They *planned* this," Roger screamed. "I'm *sure* they did."

Maria also mentioned (on her own account) getting into shape: running, starting an aerobics class; she said she'd like to dance some nights, she thought. She said she'd brought a bunch of reading she'd been putting off. She also said she had this vague idea for some . . . meetings, "sort of," maybe over at the church.

"What? Services?" said Roger.

"Hey," she said, and laughed. "You never know."

"There's just one other thing," the E-Man said, when it seemed that everyone was finished talking. "We've got some people in the band whose folks are still not sold on this, our being up here. So some of us were thinking: If we had some sort of Open House, maybe two–three weeks from now, and invited all the parents for the day or something, maybe that'd show them that it's cool up here. That what we're doing can be best described — this is what my old man likes to say — as 'quite excitingly constructive.' " And the E-Man beamed around the room. His father was some sort of shrink; E never seemed to have a hassle over anything.

People nodded back at him on this one. Seppy looked over at Maria. She interpreted that look as being "fraught" with meaning.

11

Sheriff Omar

They'd finished playing volleyball, the evening of the seventh day. There'd been one all-girl team: "The Spikèd Heels," they'd called themselves. By scoring more than seven points in every game, to go with an eight-point handicap, they'd won the river rights for afterwards. So they had gone in that direction, trailing taunts and towels.

The two male teams, "The Macho Bashos" and "The Settin' Swine" were sittin' on the porch of the hotel (Jake had made a sign: *Ye Anorexic Armes*), belly-aching back and forth about the point spread, along with other reasons why they hadn't won. Roger had a simple explanation. He'd been on the Swine, with five guys from The Guise. He said he'd known for days "they couldn't play together." Jake and Seppy, intellectuals, insisted they were thrown off by geometry: "faulty angles of deflection and the shapes of the opponents." Parmenter, who hadn't played at all, said his fellow men were smart to lose the games and thus avoid the icy river, afterwards. "That thing is sperm-bank city, man," he'd said.

They saw the Jeep come rolling up the street before they heard it. It was a CJ7 hardtop, painted black, white letters on the tires. It pulled up right beside the porch. A pair of eelskin boots slid out. Followed by a pair of creased, tan double-knits, looking soft as cashmere, and a cotton chambray shirt, light blue to match the eyes above it, possibly. His face was smooth and tan, except for smile lines on the cheeks and at the corners of those dancin' baby-blues.

"Good evenin', gen'lemen," this fellow said. "Is Seppy or Maria anywhere about?"

He must've not seen Seppy, leaning up against the porch rail, halfway hidden by a column.

"Hey," said Seppy, getting up. He looked embarrassed. "It's the sheriff. How you doin', Sheriff? Maria — she's down swimming." He turned to all the others on the porch. "This is the sheriff of Hupee County. We met him a few weeks ago." He shook his head and grinned. "Sheriff, I forget your name. I'm really sorry."

The sheriff waved that off. "Don't matter in the slightest." And he smiled from one end of the porch right to the other. "I'd be pleased if you'd just call me Omar, boys. I'm mighty glad to meet you all."

He ambled over to the porch. Put a haunch up on it. Picked a bit of twig, or straw, or splinter off the ground and slid it in a corner of his mouth. It was as if he'd joined the group. *Include me in*, his body seemed to say. He didn't have a hat on, and his thick, trimmed hair was black as polished ebony. Put that on top of smooth, brown, chiseled features, bright blue eyes, and glistening white teeth, and you've got a group of attributes most guys could stand to live with.

"How's every little thing up here, now?" he inquired of these newfound friends of his.

"Oh, fine," "Real good," and "Couldn't be better," different people said. Most of them were pretty new at sheriffs.

"That's nice," the sheriff said. "I'm really pleased to hear that." He stretched one leg and flicked a bit of lint (perhaps) from off that knee. "I just thought I'd take a swing up here and see how you were making out. Bring you the welcome of the county. Unofficially, of course."

"Well, we're really liking it," said Seppy, feeling more or less responsible for this. "And we're doing good. It's awfully *peaceful*," he said, pointedly. "You're the only person who's come up that road since we first got here. And we've been here for a week, I guess."

"Uh-huh," the sheriff said. "That's right. Well, that seems fine to me. And everybody's keeping busy? Not too homesick for the city lights, I hope." They could hear the girls coming back from the river, and he looked in that direction. The girls had started singing. It was "Losing True," that Roches song. People on the porch shook heads. To them, this sheriff sounded something like a teacher, the young and friendly kind. It was smart to take it slow with ones like that, at first, they knew. You didn't want to jump right on their laps. "No, not at all," they said. And, "This is really great." But nothing more.

The sheriff nodded, still looking toward the song-sounds.

"Uh, we've been doing some repairs," said Seppy, stuffing words into the silence. "Fixing windows. And this one roof, over there. . . ."

83

The girls appeared from around the corner of the block of buildings, more or less across the street. They were wet-heads, holding heavy towels, most of them in shorts and sweatshirts.

"I'm *losin'* you
choosin' to. . . ," they sang.

The sheriff stood for their arrival. His hands were close together near his belt, ready to start clapping, maybe. He didn't have a gun — where you could see it, anyway.

"Look who's here, Maria," Seppy called. The singing stopped. "The sheriff. *Omar*. He just drove up a little bit ago, to see how we were doing."

"Cool," Maria said. She couldn't believe the "Omar," for his name. But she didn't remember what the Sheriff Something nameplate on his desk had said. She thought he'd been a little better-looking in his uniform, but he was still by no means bad. She flipped a hand at him. "Hey, Omar."

"Howdy, ma'am," he said, and smiled, and touched a finger to his forehead. "How're things?"

"Just great," she said. "Closing in on perfect." Had he mentioned The Defenders of the Fate, she wondered? Or had Seppy?

"Been every bit as quiet as you said," she added. "We haven't seen another soul since we've been up here. Not a living body, not a fillet, not a soul." She checked the sheriff out some more, wondering what Mimimi was thinking. Probably the same as she was: Those soft tan pants of his were tighter than they had to be. She was glad she had a big old chamois shirt on.

84

"Seppy here was saying you've been fixing up some," said the sheriff. "I got to hopin' I could take a little tour while I was here. Never have done more than just drive up and down the road, before." He was looking straight at her, when he said that, his meaning absolutely clear, she thought. Like: take me.

"Sure," she said. "A trip through the facility? Why not? The tour guide presently on duty is Mimimi, here." She put an arm around the redhead's shoulders, gave a squeeze. The sheriff sucked a little breath in. "I think she's got the spiel down cold. But just in case she doesn't, I'll come, too. Prompt her if she needs it."

The sheriff looked at Mimimi, and then Maria. Then back to Mimimi again. It seemed that he was going to take the set.

"Howdy, tour guide Mimi. It'll be my pleasure," he maintained. He touched his forehead to her, too. "Shall we go, then, ladies?" he inquired. And he stuck his elbows out on either side, his meaning unmistakable.

Half amused, half feeling hustled, the girls each slid a hand in, took an arm, and let themselves be led across the street.

When they were out of earshot, Roger turned and whispered this to Seppy: "I don't think he plans on reading them their rights, do you?"

"This is where the better element in town resides, I'd say," Maria said, pointing to the block of buildings on the wooden sidewalk, the ones with storefronts in a lot of them. "Her and me, to give you two extreme examples."

85

"All the residents have *jobs*, of course," said Mimimi. "Many of them work in this same neighborhood."

"That's quite correct," Maria said. "This city is a safety net for people in our age group. Falling objects all stop here." The sheriff's head went back and forth between the two of them. He looked downright exhilarated.

She opened the first storefront door and flicked on the light. Sawdust on the floor and power tools. It was Jake and Seppy's workshop, which was presently producing "generic" platform beds for everyone who wanted/needed them.

"Upstairs, we have the Jake and Seppy Dream Suite," said Maria. "Or we will have, in a month or two."

"According to its brilliant young designers," added Mimimi, "the Dream Suite will allow a college, say, to house three kids in space they used to use for two."

"And kids will love the Dream Suite so, they'll fight for every vacancy in one," Maria said.

"Well, I'll be jiggered," said the sheriff. His tone of voice said, clearly: *I am having fun.*

"The Jake and Seppy Dream Suite," Mimimi explained, "is unisex *or* mix-and-match. One size fits all. They plan to next apply these principles to low-cost housing. Possibly in India."

"Next door, here," Maria moved, and said, "we have apartments. Some occupied, some not." His eyes had scrambled up her back, from heels to waist, lingered on the lilac legs of her short pants; her chamois shirttail didn't do him any favors. She only pointed at the door; it didn't look as if she planned to go inside.

"Now, how's that work?" the sheriff asked. "Do, like, two girls bunk in together? And then a pair of guys next door?"

"Nope. No roommates. Everybody has some private space," said Mimimi. "Good fences make good neighbors, and all that."

"Actually," Maria laughed, "we say we have apartments, but they look like cells, still. Most of us are sleeping on a mattress on the floor. No one has a bureau drawer yet. We just brought in the mattresses — they're foam — two days ago."

"Shoot," the sheriff said. "Two days ago? They can't be hardly broken in yet." And he winked at her, Maria.

Maria didn't laugh or smile or wink or speak. When in doubt, sometimes — and especially with older guys and cops — the best thing you can do is stoneface them. This sheriff rubbed the eye he'd winked with, as if he'd just had something in it, all along.

"We've got one kid up here who's taken on the job of studying careers," Maria said, moving down the sidewalk once again, away from him, and pointing at another door. "She said she really didn't know what anybody *did*, all day, except for clerks and cleaning ladies. In different *jobs*, I mean. So now she's finding out. Anyone can ask her to find out about a job they'd like to know about. She writes away for information. Like, what do people *do* who sit around at desks in banks? Or sheriffs? What do *they* do all day long?"

87

"Hey," said Omar, "can't she watch TV? We gun down bad guys, mostly. Tip our hats and act real shy around the ladies." He laughed. "That's part of the job description. We're a pretty awkward bunch of guys. Well-meaning, but inclined to foot-in-mouth disease."

"*Right*," Maria said. She guessed he meant for her to hear that as a takeback for that mattress line, almost an apology. A drop-your-guard-I'm-harmless sort of thing. Omar was a bumpkin on ball bearings: swift and silky-smooth, she thought, almost hypnotic, in a kind of way. He reminded her a bit of Noah, her constrictor.

"This is where your tour guide spends her days," Maria said, nodding at the next door, and at Mimimi. There were two signs over the door, a large square one that said "Offices of the Anti-Abulia Society," and a long skinny one that said "Mariasburg Immigration and Rationalization Services, Inc. (a subsidiary of the Anti-Abulia Society)."

Omar stood and studied them.

"This is amazing," he said. "You've got an Anti-Abulia Society up here? Me, I filled out an application to the one in San Mañana, years ago, but I put off sending it on account of I wasn't sure if what I had was an ectopic inactivity disorder or just a case of plain old country dally-dawdles." And he turned around and smiled at them.

"Check this out," Maria said. "By day, High Sheriffness of Hupee County. At night, a visiting professor of linguistics. No normal person knows the meaning of 'abulia.' How come you do, Omar?"

"Why, shucks," the sheriff said. "You didn't see my star, last time? I got that baby when I went to

State. Pure gold. An' you know what else I got?"

"Let me guess," said Mimimi. "A law degree."

"Close," he said. "A masters in psychology."

Maria whistled. Then she said, "You ought to meet my mother. She's a waitress."

As they approached the church, Omar said to Mimimi, "And what about your other work, with Immigration and Rationalization?"

"Oh, that," she said. "The Rationalization part is strictly mail order, these days. Nobody up here seems to need good reasons not to do the things they know they ought to. I had a great prospective client up and throw her cigarettes away two days ago. Pissed me off, I'll tell you. Immigration's what I work at, now. I watch the borders, keep an eye out for illegal aliens."

"Like me?" the sheriff asked.

"Nah," said Mimimi. "You may be habit-forming, Sheriff — I can't tell — but no way you're illegal. Also, you don't want to settle here."

"Suppose I did, though," Omar said. He shrugged. "Or suppose I wanted just to visit now and then — maybe spend the night. How would people feel about that? How would you two feel, for instance?" No one answered right away. He pursed his lips, then rolled his head around, as if his neck was hurting. "Hey!" he said, and pointed. "Isn't that a raven? Look!"

Maria looked at Mimimi instead, and wrinkled up her nose and did a number with her eyes: you take it.

"Yup," said Mimimi, "and you're the sheriff of the county — this is open range for both of you.

Even if nobody liked you, we'd act real nice and stay on your good side. That's important for the town, and we" — she smiled and popped her eyes — "just *love* this little town, here."

"Girl don' run a rashunizin' service just for nothin'," said Maria in an awestruck mumble. "That girl can figure what to say to *anyone*."

"Well," said Omar, looking first at one of them and then the other, "I suppose if you two *act* real nice I won't have any reason to complain one bit. Me, I always say: The *play's* the thing. You dig?" He said that smiling, in a real light tone of voice, a playful tone of voice. Maria thought that he was trying to sound more like a kid their age; just another 'burger.

They'd reached the sign outside the former church. Five days before, Maria'd found a box of letters in a cupboard in the basement of the place, and so she'd spelled out on the message board:

THE CONVENTICLE FOR
COMMON KNOWLEDGE
Meetings always possible, at 9 P.M.

"Well," the sheriff said again, "what have we here, now?" He faced the sign, his feet set wider than his shoulders, and his thumbs hooked into belt loops. Most certainly a *stance*, Maria thought.

" 'The Conventicle for Common Knowledge.' " He read it off the sign. "That must not be too big of a denomination. Can't say I've ever heard of it," he said. Although his tone of voice was much the same as it had been before, Maria got the feeling he was working at it harder.

"Who has?" she said. "It's not, like, a religion. You know the meaning of 'conventicle,' I'm sure. Uptown word for 'meeting,' right? Cool bait to get the suckers in the seats."

She'd mentioned having meetings that first night, just as a thing to do, when Boid had asked if everyone would say what they were planning on, up there. But she'd gotten the idea for what those meetings might be all about the *second* day, at lunchtime.

Boid gave her the idea, himself.

She'd told him that she'd hard-boil eggs (for salad) if he would set the tables, or if he'd rather, vice versa. He'd said that sounded great except for one small detail: neither of those things were on his "I know how to" list. She'd said, "I don't believe it. *Everyone* knows boiling eggs and setting tables. They're just common knowledge."

"Oh, yeah," he'd said. "So, let's say something's in the key of C; tell me what that means. Or if you're down in Oklahoma and you need to get to Kansas, which direction do you drive?"

She'd smiled and batted both her eyes. "I haven't a clue," she'd said.

He'd stuck his nose up in the air and told her, "There you go, then. Them's *my* common knowledge, sweetheart."

Of course some other people, overhearing, got right into it. "Common knowledge" questions filled the air — and matching ignorance, some answers.

Maria worked out the mechanics of the meetings right there on the spot. A sort of information flea market, with every item free. People could post questions that they had *or* useful answers that they knew, right up there on the old church door. Each time they met, the people would decide which ones to talk about. Roger'd said, "Sounds pretty orgiastic, yessiree. Mutual misinformation."

Of course this fellow Omar had to go right up the steps and see what sort of things were posted *then*; the girls stayed down beside the signboard. It was pretty nearly dark, and they were ready for the tour to end.

The sheriff took his time. But when he came on down, it seemed as if he'd liked what he had seen; the guy was smiling broadly.

"Very interesting," he said. "There's one or two things there I'd like to know myself."

Neither of them asked him "what?" Instead, they turned and headed for his Jeep across the way. The hotel porch was now deserted.

"A bunch of kids live here," said Mimimi, pointing to the building, finishing the tour. "It's also where the kitchen is." She stopped beside his car.

"Which, tragically, is closed," Maria said, before he could say "coffee."

The sheriff checked his wristwatch. "Looks like time for me to head on out of here," he said. "But I'm gonna take you up on that-there open invitation, maybe get in on the v-ball next time, or whatever. Hupee City's nice, but just a little bit uptight, old-fashioned, taken as a steady diet. Me, I like more of a mellow atmosphere."

He took a quick glance up and down the street.

"Well, thank'ee for the tour," he said, and moving with an easy grace at speed that any boa would admire, he kissed first Mimimi right on, and then Maria near, the mouth (she'd had that instant's warning), and hopped into his jeep.

"Oh," he said, straight at Maria, "I went and talked to Sledge. Tell you all about it, next time." And he spurted gravel, getting out of there.

Next morning, on her way to breakfast, Maria took a detour by the church, just to see what he had read, from off the door. To guess what . . . well, *impression* all the different questions/answers might have had on him, and which ones he might have an interest in, himself.

Right there in the middle, written in a brisk, authoritative hand, there was a good strong possibility:

> *What does a guy have to do to get laid around here? (And please, let's not pretend that doesn't happen.)*

12

Everybody's Problem

The second that Maria finished reading it, she ripped that question (and its trailer) off the door. She was sure that Omar was the one who'd written it, the jerk, the *asshole*. The trailer was the give-away. There were some guys — not many, one or two — who might have put that question up, just as a joke, hah-hah. But the trailer was pure adult, the language of authority: "let's not *pretend* . . . " et cetera.

If she'd left it up (she told herself) other people would have had to see it and discuss it; probably *some* people would get real upset. She thought of the line from a Dylan song: "You just kind of wasted my precious time. . . ." She wasn't going to let him do that to her, period. Oh, yeah, not much.

She went to breakfast. Took some apple juice, a bowl of granola, made a cup of tea. Ate her breakfast slowly, looking all around, but chatting, too. Real sociable. When Mimimi came in, she took a deep breath, let it out, got up, and went right over to her.

"We have to talk," she said.

Mimimi dropped her chin and looked up at her

94

out of the tops of her green eyes. She flicked her tongue against her upper lip a bunch of times, just making idiotic sounds.

"I can't," she finally said. "Not yet. My mouth is still asleep. My mind, *aussi*. Total English sentences are too much effort, still. Jus' lemme, lemme . . . *you* know." She made some feeding, drinking motions. Held up all the fingers on one hand: *gimme five*, that seemed to say.

Maria nodded. She saw some dirty dishes, took them with her own, and washed them. Put the milk back in the fridge, got some coffee grounds out of the sink, and replaced the full garbage bag inside the can with a clean new empty one. She put the full one, neatly tied, by the back door. When Mimimi picked up the last bite of toast from her plate and aimed it at her mouth, Maria, with a graceful swoop, picked up the plate and took it to the sink, where she was shortly joined by Mimimi, still drinking from her mug.

"You know who you remind me of?" Mimimi said. "My *mother*: Mrs. Punctual. The Punc Rocker, I used to call her. She'd stand over me when I was eating my breakfast, shifting her weight from one foot to the other and telling me to hurry or I'd be late for school. When I had all the time in the world. Like now. Isn't that the whole point of this place, didn't someone say?"

She looked at Maria's face. "All *right*," she said. "I'm finished. Let's go to the office."

"Well, I'm completely sure he wrote it, too," said Mimimi. "And that he meant the thing for us. But still. That doesn't mean it isn't everybody's problem. You ought to see what Seppy thinks. Me, I'm a lot more pissed than scared. Omar is a dick-head, but we've known dick-heads all our lives — right back to Dick and Jane."

"Oh, I'm not *scared*," Maria said. "The way I see it, Omar's a real mirror case. When he looks at his reflection, he *loves* seeing Sheriff Right Guard, fast man with a speed-stick. He wouldn't risk that image for a piece or two of — whatchacallit? — high school sassafras." She grinned. "Just suppose the guy contracted . . . *genital abulia*." And she overdid a shudder.

Maria felt much better. They'd been batting Omar back and forth for fifteen minutes. Omar and that question, Omar and his sleazy moves, Omar and what-next. He'd certainly be back. Neither of them doubted that. But the more they talked about him, the more ordinary he began to seem, the more like other guys they'd known. The difference was: he was the first one of that type they'd known who wore a uniform, who had his kind of power. And who had visited Mariasburg.

"Genital abulia, there's a concept," Mimimi grinned back, then frowned. "The thing that's just incredible to me is here we are, about as far away from everywhere as we can get and *still* they find us. They just won't let us alone."

"Men," Maria sighed. "I know. All my life it's been like that. I guess I just exude this animal attraction, a sort of a *penumbra*, you conceivably could say. In kindergarten — "

"Just shut up," said Mimimi. "You know I don't mean men. I mean authority. Adults who want to tell us what to do, or use us. I swear — every expedition into any trackless wilderness should pack a teenaged kid along. In case."

"In case of what?" Maria said.

"In case they get completely lost," said Mimimi. "All they'd have to do then is take out the teenager and right away there'd be some sort of lech or guidance person on the scene to tell the kid exactly what to do, and where, and naturally, how often. And so, that easily, the expedition would be found and saved."

"You think I ought to talk to Seppy, though, about — *you* know — the Omar thing in general?" Maria asked.

"And that question in particular," said Mimimi. "See what he says. It couldn't hurt. If Omar does keep coming back — and we both know he will — it won't be only us that have to deal with him."

". . . sure I do," said Seppy. "I know you didn't mean it like he took it — *probably*. It's just what you two do — *can* do. I saw the start of your routine. Kids would know you weren't serious, but people Omar's age. . . ."

Maria looked down at him. She was perched up on a platform in his workshop. They could hear The Guise rehearsing from across the way. Jake was somewhere working on a painting; Sep was sawing, drilling, bolting: making bed frames.

"You're nuts," Maria said. "Meem and I don't tease; you're talking trash. He offered us an arm, we took it, end of story. Omar is a dick-head. We never gave him anything but sass and stare-downs."

"Well, maybe he thought that was cute, or something," Seppy mumbled. "And I remember you told

Mee he was an eight point six. Those aren't dick-head numbers, Mya."

"Seppy, listen," said Maria. "You're not making sense. If Omar thought that Mee and I were hot for him, why would he bother, even, with the church door bit? The Martin Luther number. To me, that *proves* what I've been saying, that all he got from us was frostbite."

Seppy seemed to chew on that, while he abused the country air with SkilSaw sounds.

"You got a point," he finally said. "Assuming that he wrote the document in question." He held a hand up, just before she would have spoken. "Which I completely do." He grinned. "Hey, all us local boys know all we have to do is lose a game or two of volleyball, and pretty soon some chick'll feel so sorry for us that she'll break into our room and . . . and spike us good. Or whatever. You get the general idea, I'm sure." He shrugged, looking (so Maria thought) delighted with himself.

"*Spike us good?*" she said. "You're sickening, you know that? Pathetic, in a rural-grade-school sort of way. You think we women want to be like guys? That I, for one, would ever want to be like *you?*" She cocked her head. "You know, I almost wish I *could* be you, for about twenty-four hours." She smiled a thoughtful, evil smile. "I'd show you things you can't even imag — "

"Oh, sure," he interrupted. "Here's our little Doctor Ruthette, junior. Sure." He stuck his tongue out at her. "But if you can stand to return to the original subject, Lotharia, how about the question of the question? *I* still think you ought to bring it up. Let everybody have the poop on Omar. Seems to me the other women here would *want* to know."

"Well, yeah, maybe," she said. "But I hate to bother people, just when everyone is getting settled down. Why stir things up?" She looked away; her fingers found and traced the platform's plywood grain.

"I don't think you're being fair, if you don't tell them. You'd be treating them like children," Seppy said. He put down the saw, came over to her, and rested his chin on the platform's edge, with his hands on either side of it. She began to stroke his hair.

"People didn't come up here to drop out of the human race," he said. "If this place does anybody any good, it'll be because it's given them some time, like you've been saying. But time for what? Not *just* for deciding about the future. There's other major stuff to think about. Like, what matters and what doesn't, to a halfway decent person. We're all living here together. Well, what does that mean? Do we owe each other anything at all? Omar has a certain kind of attitude; how should we react to that? It's *everybody's* problem. You *must* see what I'm saying."

"Sure, of course I do," Maria said. She smiled at him, her hand now on his cheek. "Mimimi agrees with you. And you said the same thing the very first night. You want us all to care for one another. So do I. Everybody doin' it for everybody else." She let herself fall over on the platform, so she was lying on her side, her lips not far from his.

"Sepperino." She just breathed the word. "You know I want that, too. But where's it come from, atmosphere like that? You can't send out for it, like pizza. Maybe all that everyone can do is give it." She was whispering. "And live it."

Seppy smiled, and reached, and smoothed Maria's long, dark hair.

"Truth," he whispered back, puckering his lips to make the word. Maria kissed him then, loving him with all her heart. She'd tell the Omar story that same night, at dinner; she'd just decided that.

13

Truth Hostel

" '. . . let's not pretend that doesn't happen,' " read Maria. She looked around the room. "I'm pretty sure that Omar wrote it — that sheriff who was here?"

Willa'd made them spinach pies for dinner. People had been blown away by them. Far from being solid spinach, the things were also full of seasoned meat and different kinds of cheese and spices, all inside a mashed potato crust. So for dessert, Maria thought, why not sleaze and crackers?

"Well, do we know the guy's *address*?" asked Roger. "How does a person get in *touch* with him?"

"As soon as I saw him," Sookie said, "he reminded me of this guy I know back in town who used to. . . ."

For the next ten minutes, a lot of people joked, told stories, gave opinions and suggestions and solutions, some of them unworkable, to say the least. Maria thought the females in the room seemed angry, for the most part, but one or two looked ill at ease and undecided. She knew she'd had the same expression on *her* face a bunch of times when she was wondering if something or some person in her life was really worth the hassle.

Some of the guys refused to get involved at all, it seemed. Except for an occasional one-liner, they were silent, listening, many of them looking at the floor, a table top, their folded hands. Maria wasn't sure what they were thinking. *Not my problem? Much ado about nothing? Better not to mess with country sheriffs who had county jails, with maybe soundproofed basement rooms in them?*

"Well," said Mimimi, at last, "I'm against confronting him at all. We haven't any proof, so he could just act dumb." She dropped her voice to deep and idiotic. " 'What question?' he could say. It isn't like he wrote it on a parking ticket."

"I agree," said Etta. She had come with Parmenter. She had a way of tilting up her chin and looking side to side, a small smile on her lips. That and a gorgeous, massy mane of coal-black hair, and perfect skin and ditto almond eyes, "and *cheekbones*," the green-eyed Mimimi would always say.

"What I intend to do," she quietly informed the room in measured, mellow tones, "is just pretend the man does not exist. No law that says a person has to interact with sheriffs."

"You're right," said Mimimi. "Although the *ideal* thing would be if we could go on being sort of friends with him. In his opinion, anyway. Omar has his usefulness, let's face it."

"His usefulness?" said Etta. She raised one slender, arcing eyebrow, and she did that smile of hers. "For what?"

And the next thing that Maria knew, it was the

Mimimi-Tells-Untold-Stories Time. Her subject: The Defenders of the Fate.

She told about them more or less in outline form, Maria thought. About the night so many weeks before when she and Seppy'd stayed in Jacks-'r-better, and what they'd found there on the message board concerning "Satan pedermasters." And what the sheriff said about the cult — its tendencies and so on — and how he'd said he'd more or less look out for all of them and for their town. Protect them from the weirdos, so to speak.

The only trouble was: She told all that as if she was reminding everyone about a thing they'd known before but had forgotten. She said: "*You* know . . ." a lot. She just *assumed* Maria'd told that story lots of times, to everyone.

When Mimimi was finished, people started buzzing right away, turning to the others at their tables. Maria thought she heard the question "Did you. . . ?" answered quite a lot by "No, did *you?*" Mimimi turned half-around in her direction, wearing what Maria knew to be her *uh-Oh* face.

Soon, Maria saw, a lot of people switched their heads around to look at *her*, and threw out different questions starting with "How come. . . ?"

It was a rotten, rotten moment. Maria would have liked to have been elsewhere, anywhere — back in Mr. Godfrey's office, saying, "I won't take the money; shove it." But seeing as she wasn't, she stood up and faced it, them, the music.

"Stomp me, tromp me, I won't blame you. Stake me out in lion country, covered up with lamb chops. I'm joking but I'm serious; I *stink*," she said. "I didn't have the guts, the common decency . . . no, that's not it, exactly. I just didn't respect everyone enough to tell them what I knew and let them make their own decisions." She was getting emotional, and she just hoped her voice would stay together.

"I guess I wanted this damn town too much, and was afraid that you . . . *you* know," she said. "So I did exactly what *they* do" — she waved a hand: out there — "and what I'm always dumping on them for. There's no excuse for what I did — not telling you about those guys. What can I say? I'm really, really sorry."

She sat down fast. She knew her face was red and she could feel her eyes begin to burn. But she'd said what she believed, and that was something, for a weak-kneed hypocrite (she told herself).

There was that awkward silence an apology can bring. Maybe nothing's settled, but anger seems a bit . . . unsuitable. Seppy jumped right in, then. What a buddy, what a pal.

"*I* could have said something, too," he said. "I knew all that stuff. I'm just as much to blame as she is. This isn't an excuse, but it's the truth. I thought: Why bother telling anyone about some so-called 'danger' that they'll more than likely never even hear about, much less have to face? I can see I was wrong, for the reasons she said, but I really didn't think we were putting anyone in danger."

Babe had raised his hand. He just was sitting there, not showing any feelings, like impatience, with his arm held high. He was looking at Maria, so she did what he was asking her to do; she nodded.

The guy stood up, all six foot four of him, two forty-five. He had a shock of colorless blond hair, and light blue eyes that often seemed unoccupied.

"I would rather have known about those people myself." He spoke slowly, clearly, in a pleasant, inexpressive voice. "But if I had, I also would have come here, anyway. This is too beautiful a thing to let yourself be scared away from, especially by people — just as Seppy said — you probably will never have to deal with. Being with this group up here has been the best part of my life, so far."

There were a bunch of "yeahs" when Babe sat down, and also handclaps, here and there.

"I know I'm getting *my* money's worth," said Roger.

The E-Man jumped up next.

"Well, I guess it's common knowledge now, that Maria isn't perfect," he said. "But as my father often says, perfection is a bore. Which reminds me, if anyone noticed that the first floor bathroom wasn't clean today. . . . Well, er, that was mine and I forgot — no kidding — and I'll do it just as soon as this is over."

That seemed to start another buzz. Friends consulted one another, but the tone had changed. A lot of people in the room were — anyway — *half* smiling at Maria and at Seppy.

"Okay," said Roger, loudly. "Just making sure I have this straight. . . . Here's what we've decided so far, right? First, bugger the sheriff, but not so he will notice it. Second, E-Man, for his penance, gets to do the cans all month." He grinned. "And *that* reminds me of the Open House, I don't know why. But according to my Daily Aid, it's just ten days away. So if we want to keep this world from ending then, for some of us, don't you think we — "

"Oh, yikes," cried Willa. "I forgot. My parents want to bring my *aunt*. Can I just tell them we don't have. . . ."

And so the subject of the Open House was then discussed at length, and plans were slowly made; no one seemed at all inclined to hurry through the process. In fact, and to the contrary, ice cream was called upon, eventually, to make sure that hunger-faintness didn't cost them any good ideas. When dinner cleanup finally started, it was past eleven; everybody helped and got it done in no time. But E-Man, he forgot to do the can, again.

When Maria finally drifted to her room, she didn't know exactly what to think. Except that Seppy had been right about the truth and, somehow, people had forgiven her.

So, the next night, there was Omar back in town again as big as life. But earlier than last time, and dressed for volleyball in dark blue sweats with wide white piping on the sides and a light gray t-shirt with the words (Roger almost choked) "Hupee County Vice" on it. They were having pick-up, mixed-up teams, and he joined in and proved to be . . . outstanding. He wasn't just good at volleyball, he also was completely *charming*, praising other people's shots and efforts, playing down his own. The only proposition anybody heard him make was "Let me get it" when a badly mis-hit serve (no, not his own, of course) went sailing off and rolled on down the hill.

Afterwards, he walked back to the Armes and sat out on the porch and drank some lemonade with everyone. He had three glasses of the stuff, and with each glass he sat down in a different place, with different people. When he was finishing the third — the crowd had thinned way out by then — he finally made his way to where Maria was. Mimimi had gone inside, already.

"Hey," he said to her. "What happened to your podner? Don't you two always play together?" He might have winked; Maria wasn't sure. The guy had tricky eyes.

"Not always," she replied.

"That sure was fun," he said. "I *do* love volley-ball. Seems to me that everyone is having one great time up here."

"You got it," said Maria. "We is pigs in slop."

"So, when are 'common knowledge' meetings, anyway?" asked Omar. "Could it be possible there's one tonight?"

"Nope," Maria said. "We met last night. There were a bunch of interesting questions. It was good."

"Oh, yeah?" the sheriff said. "But how about the answers? Were there any answers that a guy like me might want to know about?"

"I doubt it," said Maria. "Not unless you're weak on CPR or starting fires, or the basics of the Jewish or the Catholic faiths."

The sheriff's face did, like, a little twitch. Then he smiled and crossed himself, but all ass-backwards, crazily.

"That doesn't sound too personal," he said.

"It isn't and it wasn't," said Maria. "Personals belong in magazines or papers. We don't get into trash like that." She stood up then, and started walking toward the hotel door. She'd liked the way her voice had sounded, totally offhand.

107

"O-kay," he said. He sighed and followed her. "So maybe I've misread the situation here. I guess I should apologize. But heck, *I* didn't know. And mama always said it never hurts to ask. Maybe if we got to know each other some. . . ."

She turned, a half-smile on her lips. Talk about persistent ego-cases. But Omar kept on talking.

". . . and meanwhile I got news. About a favor that I've done you, just for nothing. See? I *can* be nice. Like I said the other night, I went and saw ol' Sledge," he said. Maria made a face.

"I told him what I could about this place," said Omar. "All good stuff, of course. And I made it clear I wouldn't tolerate no fussin'. No trespassing or threats, no *tactics*, as he likes to call them. Well, of course he didn't say straight out that he'd be good, because according to him the only law they recognize is God's. Or how they read it, anyway. When you believe that Armageddon's right around the corner, there isn't a whole hell of a lot else that you're concerned about. But he did say that he'd take what I explained about your town under advisement, pending his own further study of the matter. Well, I told him he'd better do that from a distance, not up close — apparently, some of them were here one time, before you got set up — and he said he thought he could, aided by his 'revelations,' as he calls them, which are these messages from God he says he gets. But what might really help is if I brought someone from the town up there one day to talk with him — show him what you're like. I said maybe we'd work that out, and that's the way we left it."

Maria looked at him. "You think that that'll satisfy the guy?" she said. "If some of us went over there and talked to him about ourselves and why we came up here — that kind of thing?"

"It might," said Omar. "Probably not *some* of you, specifically. I'd recommend a committee of one, someone articulate, like you — no kidding. The Defenders are a little goosey when it comes to company; they think the outside world is spying on them all the time. But one person, if I brought her — a woman's much less threatening to them, given their beliefs — that might work. You're only one of Adam's lesser ribs, to Sledge." He grinned.

"Well," Maria said. "I'll think about it. Sure." Her understanding was that everyone wanted to make use of Omar, and here he was, attempting to be useful. And it surely was a fact she owed the other kids a little usefulness, herself.

"Sure." The sheriff echoed her. He stuck his hand out. "And meanwhile I'll just try to be a friend of yours, and everybody else's here — no fooling."

She shook with him. That seemed okay; a neutral, only *slightly* friendly thing to do. He didn't try to hold her hand; he looked sincere — reformed and honest. And he walked away from her right off, whistling, and got into his Jeep, and started down the road.

Maybe he's not all that bad, she thought. Perhaps the guy was just an ordinary dick-head after all.

14

Choices

The next few days, Maria threw a lot of juice into the preparations for the Open House. She tried to put herself inside a pants or jogging suit and see Mariasburg the way a parent might — then change it. Find all the fault she could, pick up every little nit from off the body of the place, or add nice, homey little touches. The signs on bathroom doors, for instance, which used to say just "It," were taken down, replaced with "Gentlemen" or "Ladies." She made sure that there were shades on all the windows of the parents' rooms, and that they had sufficient quilts and blankets there to warm the coldest feet. She made a giant ink pad and got everyone to step on it and leave their footprint on a piece of art pad paper. Underneath each one, in crayon, she wrote the kid's first name and present weight, and posted all of them along the halls. She also heaved great sighs a lot and chewed the inside of her mouth, two things she'd hardly ever done before.

"I'm fussing like your great-aunt Fran," she said to Mimimi.

"Closer to my mom, I'd say," her friend replied. "You're up there with the great ones, girl."

"Oh, thanks a *lot*," Maria said.

She also started running harder workouts, not just for conditioning, but so she'd be too pooped to think (or worry) by the time she went to bed.

Omar showed up every other after-supper-time, and kept on acting like an Eagle scout with applications out to seminary. One night, while playing volleyball, he asked if it would be all right for him to visit during Open House. He said he'd wear his uniform and blow a little sunshine at the parents, speaking from a law-and-order point of view. Everybody looked at everybody else and said that sounded "fab."

One evening, when she felt the need to get away from everyone, Maria climbed into the belfry of the church, up to her crow's nest there, and pulled the ladder up behind her, closing the trapdoor as well. She sat there on a mattress, feeling far away from sheriffs, Open Houses — everything — and watched the darkness slowly fill the valleys. It was amazing how much longer it stayed light where she was. That thought so pleased her she flopped over on her side and fell asleep in seconds.

She woke up hearing music and stayed very still. At first, she thought she was in bed in her apartment in the town, though no one near her ever played their music loud enough at night so she could hear it. Then she realized she wasn't *there*, but where she was, inside the church's tower, high up in her special place. The music came from one flight underneath her. The music *and* the voices, too: a man's voice and a woman's.

She tried to hear what they were saying, who they were. She knew it wasn't Mimimi and someone.

Mee would have seen the ladder wasn't in the room —
and left. They'd made a deal on that.

She caught her first intelligible words; the pair
below had raised their volume slightly and for emphasis, it seemed.

". . . awful damn remote," the girl's voice said.

"Much too fucking serious . . ." the guy threw
in on top of it.

Moving very slowly, so as not to make the slightest sound, Maria got her head above the rope-hole
and looked down. There was no way she could keep
herself from doing that. Or, then, from soundless-
saying just: *oh-shit, oh-shit, oh-shit, oh-shit* . . . on
and on, repeatedly, inside her head.

They'd lighted Mimimi's four yellow candles, and
they'd put the candle holders on the floor around
the mirror (lady's dressing-table type, with plastic
handle, pink). On the mirror were the four white
powder lines, and the Eurhythmics did their mellow
background duty from a little Sanyo box. Of course,
he used a rolled-up twenty and went first; of course,
she smiled and licked her lips before she took her
turn. And, unsurprisingly, he then laid back and let
her lead the expedition, the one where she sets out
to find what he was sure she would agree was quite
a treasure.

Maria sank down on her mattress once again;
she did that just as silently as she had moved before.
She didn't want to see, and she was very glad she
couldn't hear too terribly specifically. But even so,
it wasn't hard to keep her place in what was going
on down there. Or to come to the conclusion that
she hated all these things: listening, the way she felt,
the circumstances, the deception, them. Or, not en-

tirely *them*. She knew the reason that she hadn't moved or made some other sound was . . . well, that one of them was Sookie. Who maybe wasn't having all that great a time, herself.

Pretty soon, Maria heard them leaving, going down the stairs.

The boy was one of those who'd come up with The Guise, as boyfriend of a girl named Noralee, a singer with the group. His name was Converse; he was big, and really not a blond and (very, very) Bad.

Converse, known as Connie, was a looker, give him that. *He* did. He gave himself full credit, and he never kept his riches from the public. While other people sunbathed near the river (just for instance), Connie got his rays right by the hotel porch, lolling in a chaise in his unlined bikini, always right about the time that people came to lunch. ("Talk about a human diet pill," said Mimimi one day, while passing, loud enough so he could hear. But Connie only smiled. He knew that she was funnin' — had to be.)

He thought he was a singer. He'd also thought that Noralee, who *was* a singer, could arrange to get him in The Guise. She'd gotten him a tryout once, and he had been turned down, by secret ballot. He'd figured that was out of jealousy, or strangeness; besides, he'd had a cold. The lead male singer with The Guise had no appeal; anybody who could see knew that. Connie's backup plan was also simple: he would stay with Noralee until he got another tryout with the band, and they all saw the error of their ways and took him in. At that point he would dump her. It was better to be unattached when you were singing lead and playing dates at lots of different places for so many different fans, and fannies. In the meantime, he just planned to hang around the band a lot; give them all a chance to get to know him better. He'd help them move and get set up and be real helpful in a lot of other ways. Like give them feedback on their new material, offer little insights and suggestions.

What he hadn't counted on was just how monstro-fucking-boring this Mariasburg would be. There was nothing that resembled life or action; except the food was better, he could have been in jail, he thought. Everybody worked their ass off, grinned, and said that this was heaven. Noralee was less . . . agreeable, you could say — always seemed to have to work, or get her sleep, or exercise.

At last, and luckily for him, he'd met this one kid, Sookie, who believed in having fun, who had a little spirit of adventure, still. And who also knew exactly how to treat a guy, who knew she couldn't only take, take, take, and never give.

Maria, in the next day's early morning light, got up, threw water on her face, and reached for a scowl. No sweat, she found a black one, put it on along with running clothes, and did some stretches on the floor beside her bed. Then she headed out to run (down certain sun-splashed logging roads) to try to clear her head. The things she'd seen and heard the night before, and what they meant, and what they meant she'd have to *do*, were messing with her mind. Her own-a-town scenario had not, for sure, included any crap like this.

Puke-a-duke, let's see. . . . Maria breathed the thin, sweet air, settled in a running rhythm. Clearly, doing coke up there was not just private process, feeler's choice; a person doing coke could not insist "It's only me I'm hurting, man." They knew, the same as she or anybody else did, how a single solitary drug bust would affect a funky little teenaged town. The End; we'll see you; there you go; *Adios.* They knew that and they simply hadn't cared. They'd put their fun ahead of everybody else's lives and futures. Lovely little couple. Breed 'em and you'd get another Star Wars research guy, most likely.

Of course (Maria made herself admit) there wasn't any written rule that they had broken. Miss Utopia herself had seen to that: refusing to have any "rules" at all. But still, there was what Parmenter had mentioned, what he'd called a "social contract." Wasn't there? Didn't they have understandings, stuff that people understood they'd do, or wouldn't do, for everybody's sake? Like leaving any drugs at home, for instance? *Of course* they did. But those two didn't give a shit. About anyone or anything. Cheating on a girlfriend? Trespassing, et cetera, on other people's private space? No big deal — get serious. You're talking stop signs on an empty road at night. What's the big excitement, man?

Maria shook her head. *How could they?* (she thought next). *After all I've done for them* (implied).

But that thought stopped her in her tracks.

Oh, yuk! (her whole insides cried out). *What's happening to me?*

She started walking, with her chin down on her breastbone. She gave herself a slap on one bare thigh, and then the other.

115

A-ha! She thought she saw, and had the explanation, ugly as it seemed. She'd gone to bed the night before with one thought in her mind: those two would have to leave the town; they *had to* go. But she'd also been afraid she couldn't get it up to tell them. And so-o-o when she'd waked up this morning, she'd started in to make the whole deal something *personal.* If she could fix it so she hated both of them — she, poor little Martha Martyr, girlish victim of the Mob — *then* getting rid of them would be a breeze. Can't I throw the switch *now*, warden? *Please?*

But the real truth was: It wasn't personal at all. The truth was she felt *bad* for Sookie, who she liked. (Connie? Color him pathetic.) Sookie had been trying, part-time, anyway. No, this had more — like, everything — to do with *principle.*

Maria sat down on a stump. She was starting to feel better; things were getting clear. Principle was comfortable, home base. She thought that, by and large, most kids were clear on principles — the things that mattered — good at telling them apart from all the little crap that adults fussed about. Of course (to be completely fair) sometimes kids refused to make a (proper) fuss *about* their principles, which laid them open to the charge of being "immature," or "irresponsible."

But never mind all that. That wasn't her, not now. In this case she would be mature, responsible — and fussy. To double-check, she'd even run her plan by Mimimi or Seppy. Then sweetly, gently, and without the smallest vestiges of martyrdom or rage, she'd tell that pair of flamers they were history.

* * *

116

By the time Maria did her warm-down exercises, showered, and shampooed, it was just about the end of breakfast. She hustled over to the dining room and there, to her surprise, was Sookie, sitting at a table near the door, alone. Waiting, she found out. And just for her.

"Hi," said Sookie, total smiles. "I'd just about convinced myself I'd missed you. Or you'd started on a fast, or something."

"No way," Maria said with equal cheerfulness. "Food and I have got a big thing going. I really think I couldn't live without it, as they say."

Sookie looked at her and thought that over. Then she laughed. "You're a scream," she said. "You really are. But look, you want to get your breakfast, first? I've got a favor that I want to ask you."

"Sure," Maria said, thinking: this is really weird. A favor? She went for toast with peanut butter, a banana, tea. They sat down in the nearly empty room. "What's up?" she said to Sookie.

"Well, the thing is," Sookie said, "I've got this dental problem. I gotta have a root canal. I didn't want to bring it up before, 'cause — well — I thought you maybe wouldn't want me to come up here. Not that it's contagious." Sookie laughed. "But just that — I don't know — if I had to, like, go back and forth a lot, that might not be too cool. But anyway, what I had to ask you was: I need a ride to town and — well — I thought you might be going, getting ready for the Open House and all. Or that you'd know someone who was."

"Hmmm, let's see," Maria said, all stall, trying to stretch it out, get balanced up. Was this true,

117

what she was hearing? "I'm not completely sure, but Seppy's taking this week's food run. . . ."

"Oh, that'd be fantastic," Sookie said, nodding, smiling. "So he'll be going in his . . . *camper*, like? 'Cause I think I heard this other kid who said he had to go — his uncle died or something — and that way there'd be, like, space for both of us."

"It seems to me somebody else did talk to me about a ride," Maria said. "If I can just think who it was. . . ."

"I think the kid's named Connie," Sookie said. "The one *I* mean. Something like that. Big blond guy." She smiled again and dropped her eyes. "Kind of a hunk?"

"Uh-huh," Maria said. "That Connie — sure it was. And how long is it that you think you'll have to stay down there?"

"I don't exactly know," said Sookie, real off-handedly, eyeballs wandering away. "Probably just a few days. I think the dentist said he'd have to check out what he'd done a time or two." She made a face. "Believe me, I do dread it."

Yes, Maria thought, that was just the way that Sookie'd do it. Not say it right straight out; tell her one thing, mean another.

"The truth is," she said slowly, "you're not planning to come back. You've traded in your whole-grain bread for California cornflakes."

She wasn't close to being ready for the change in Sookie's face, though.

"What?" she said. "Of course I am. I sure as hell *am* coming back. What's that crack meant to mean? Are you some sort of a mind reader, or something?

Of course I'm coming back, why wouldn't I? I really love it here."

"You're lying through your Panamas," Maria told her calmly. "I think you like it here, all right, but Connie's talked you into leaving — Connie and his little bag of blow. Your needing dental work's a crock. You just didn't want to tell me you were splitting, probably for good. If all goes well with the candy man."

"That's bullshit," Sookie said. "Fuck you, Maria. Look, I'll leave my ring with you, for whachacallit." She started pulling off the little ring she always wore: slender gold around a single pearl, a little girl's ring. "Or maybe I won't go at all." Her voice had risen in defiance, to a whine; she sounded five years younger.

"No, you're going, both of you," Maria said. "Looks like it's by mutual agreement. But *I* say you're not coming back, neither of you are." She paused. "I'm sorry. Really sorry. I thought that you were getting into it."

"But wait — I am, I really am," said Sookie in that little childish voice, still. "I just needed, like, a little break, a few days off, maybe a week. . . ." But Maria only shook her head.

They sat there for a moment, looking at each other. Sookie's face got red, but then the color faded quickly.

"I bet you're sorry, bitch," she said. Her voice was very different. Then she did a namby-pamby mimicking of what Maria'd said. " 'You thought that I was getting into it.' Don't make me laugh. This place is total bullshit. You think it's cool, but what it is is one big fake, like, totally unreal. No one's free up here unless they do exactly what you say. The second that they don't and start to act, like, *normal*, nobody can stand it. Well, just because you've got a million bucks, that doesn't mean you get to jerk *my* life around. You're goddamn right we're leaving here for good." She'd gotten up. "Accent on the *good*." She was crying then, her face all red again, this time because of that, and fury. "But you're not telling me, I'm telling *you*." She was screaming. "I'll never be so glad to leave a place in my entire fucking life." And she stomped on out the door.

Maria sat there, feeling tingly inside. And terrible. So this is what it feels like (she informed herself) on the *up*-side of a confrontation, when *you* have all the power. Before, there'd always been a teacher or a parent (or a cop) whose *job* it was. Her role had been to (merely) disapprove and walk away, not get involved. "Someone better *do* something . . ." or "Frankly, what I hope is that he *does* get caught, maybe for his own sake. . . ." Those were pretty standard it-ain't-me-babe lines.

Now she had presumed to exercise some power over someone else. Someone who was not an eight-year-old with nothing more than bedtime in the balance. Someone who now hated her and thought she was . . . a different kind of person than before.

"Shit," she said out loud, as she got up. Having money, she decided, wasn't all that great. Of course it wasn't money that she meant.

She headed out the door to talk to Seppy.

*   *   *

120

"Sure, I'll take 'em. You were right," he said. "If you hadn't said exactly what you did, we'd be ass-deep in dope by the day after Open House. Chances are, it won't be only parents coming up, you know. And you can bet your life a lot of people know that Connie has it — had it — whatever. I feel bad about Sookie, too, but I remember what you said *she* said, when you first talked to her. How she'd probably be the same wherever she was. That's what they call a self-fulfilling prophecy, I guess."

"But she really was doing good," Maria said. "If instead of saying what I did, I'd just said — "

"No. Forget it," Seppy said. "She knew what she was doing, and it wasn't just the coke. Connie may be a bastard, but Sookie isn't five years old. She was choosing him for company. We're talking rotten-apple power, Mya — just what you described before, remember? And besides," he added, "it's done now, and she wouldn't stay if we begged her."

Maria knew that he was right, about the last part, anyway. The word'd get around, and maybe that'd do some good in the long run. But something Seppy'd said still bugged her. If other kids *would* get their friends to bring up dope, if they thought that they would "get away with it," or if "it didn't matter," or if "she didn't seem to care," how did that make them so different from the Sookies of this world? Or even Connie? Were they the only ones with principles?

But then she thought that maybe Seppy'd fallen into . . . kind of like a power trap. The assumption that he'd made was typical of . . . well, Carmelo High. Teachers thought that kids would *always* make

121

the worse choice rather than the better, if they had a choice at all. She didn't think that. About anybody, really. Not even Edwin Meese. Seven out of ten times, maybe — but not "always."

Maria wandered off. She felt a little giddy.

15

Weird

"Question me this answer," Maria said to Mimimi. It was four days later. They were sitting tailor-fashion on top of tables out on the wooden sidewalk in front of the offices of the Anti-Abulia Society. They were hemming tablecloths by hand. The next day was Open House, and the cloths, if they got finished, were so that everyone would have something under their plates and cups and bowls and glasses, a kind of common ground, an element of harmony. That was the theory, anyway. If they got finished. Besides, they'd finished doing every other thing that they could think of. "Ready? The answer is: When the sun don't set on Tuesdays."

"Easy," Mimimi replied. "That'd be: 'When will I ever stop spending a wildly disproportionate amount of my lifetime trying to get on the good side of people I may not even particularly like?' "

"Not bad," Maria said. "Though the *correct* question was: 'When will it be safe for us to put our girlish virtues and accessories in charming Sheriff Omar's law-abiding hands?' "

Mimimi glanced up, then made her eyes fly open, in commercial-strength amazement. "You mean the new, all-purpose Omar, with gentle bonding action?" she inquired.

"The same," Maria said. "The one I saw The Talon Man himself go arm-around-the-shoulder with, while calling him 'Big O.' "

"What?" said Mimimi. "It's come to that? *Roger* mingling with sheriffs?"

"More than mingling," Maria said. "I hate to be the one to tell you this, but — well — I saw the two of them go upside down inside the front of Rog's red Camaro. There was the sound of giggling. Dirty carburetor jokes, I hope. It might be worse."

Mimimi's full lips went tight. "Omar is using MB88; I'm sure of it," she said. "Up-to-date male bonding, state-of-the-art stuff. That sheriff knows what works, in small communities or large. For brighter, cleaner friendships every time. It shows the boys how much you have in common."

"And it isn't even filling," said Maria.

"Certainly tastes great," her friend agreed.

"And did you notice Thursday morning, when he showed up on his quote-unquote 'day off'. . . ," Maria started.

". . . how he made another beeline for the handy-*man* activities?" said Mimimi. "Why, yes. To think we *ever* thought he had designs on any of the . . . *quiff* — is that the word? — up here."

"We must have been *imagining*," Maria said.

"What silly *geese* we were," said Mimimi. "What bimbos."

"Jake told me Omar knew a lot about electric stuff and radios. Said he really could un-short a circuit," said Maria. "Or words to that effect."

"And Sep said he was sure at home with power tools," said Mimimi.

"That *boy*! He *would* be," said Maria.

"Let's just hope the *parents* are impressed with all the skills we're learning — all the down-to-earth, hands-on experience we're having, right?" said Mimimi.

"Perhaps you shouldn't say 'hands-on,' " Maria said. "But down-to-earth sounds good. Back to the soil instead of worldly. Who wouldn't want their kid to know Ten Steps to the Tomato of Tomorrow?"

"You know something?" said Mimimi. "In just the little time since I came up here, all that stuff has gotten so much more important to me. Nature, I'm referring to. Don't laugh. Dirt and trees and watching stuff begin to grow, like in the garden. Seeing all the birds and different animals. It makes me feel like more a part of something that makes sense and has some permanence. It's just a feeling — I don't know."

"Yeah," Maria said. "I know exactly what you mean. You can get the same feeling from kissing — I'm serious — when it's world-class kissing, right? You know what I mean? Or from a real hard workout, sometimes, when you feel these different parts and places in your body, and they're really fired-up and working, and you know you're getting stronger. . . . It's like you've gotten down to basics and it kind of makes you say 'Thank God, at least there's *that*. . . .' "

"I know," said Mimimi. "I think I'll end up doing something really *basic*, after this year. Something with that same right feeling to it. I'll go to college first, I hope, but after that. . . ."

"I wouldn't just do kissing, though," Maria said. "You know — full-time. Career-wise, kissing has its limitations."

Mimimi flapped the tablecloth at her. "You know what I mean," she said. "I'm serious."

"Sure," Maria said. "But weren't you before?"

"I guess," said Mimimi. "I still feel different, though. I think I do. Maybe it's just wishful thinking. Or living here without adults around. And Omar around. And having to think about this place and the parents. *And* Sookie and Connie."

Maria nodded. They'd gone quietly, Sookie and Connie. Sookie had stuck to her tooth fairytale, and Connie'd just gone; he'd really planned to, anyway. Somebody said he'd told Noralee he missed the beach too much, or had Australia in his system, couldn't get it out — some feeble thing. After he'd left, a lot of different people told Maria that was good, that he'd been doing drugs up there. She'd said to each of them she guessed that that was "common knowledge"; they'd said "yes." She'd said that someone should have brought it up, or done something about it. A couple said they'd tried.

Mimimi knew the whole straight story, of course. She'd seen the signs of someone in her little room, and Maria would have told her anyway. Mimimi had said "Poor you," and stroked Maria's hair. *She* hadn't known that Connie was a druggie, either — any more than Seppy had. It seemed that "everybody" thought if Mimimi or Seppy knew, they'd tell Maria, and then *she'd* have to do something. Mimimi found out that "everybody" felt Maria

126

wouldn't have a choice, once she learned that drugs were being used by someone. *They* had a choice, apparently, but not Maria.

"You're getting weird," Maria said. "*I* think it's tube withdrawal." And she laughed. "When you don't watch your soaps, you just forget what life is all about."

"I think that being weird may help a person to make better choices. Look at all the kids up here. A lot of them are weird in different ways," said Mimimi. "Don't you think that's possible?"

"I don't know," Maria said. She remembered Seppy, too, had mentioned weirdness to her, long ago — her subsidizing other people's weirdness. "Probably not. Maybe a little. It *could*." She put a finger up against her head. "Is it being weird that helps me make good choices? Or is it the good choices that I've made that make me weird? Sounds like the chicken or the egg. A menu problem." She laughed. "I'll throw that one at Sis next time I see her — like tomorrow."

"She *always* gave you choices, didn't she?" said Mimimi.

"Hell, yes," Maria said. "A waitress makes a mega-perfect mother."

16

Open House

"What many of you kids don't seem to realize," the father said, "is that America was *built* on competition, acquisition, and aggresh . . . *siveness*."

He looked around the room, the dining room, making sure of everyone's attention and respect. He'd thought of going into teaching once — also the Marine Corps — but had bagged both possibilities for basically the same good reason: why break ass for bread crusts? (Also, what he'd heard, these big Samoan kids'd catch you going home from school and cut you up and put you in the cookpot, if they took a notion to.) But still he liked to talk about America to kids — read off the ingredients that, mixed with guys like him, could put some real good numbers on the board.

He was a man of ample girth who wore a small mustache above an old "Nice Try, Chernobyl" t-shirt — an electrical contractor. He'd started as a one-man shop just eighteen years before and now was bidding on apartment houses, shopping center jobs, and the White House Christmas tree. He'd tell you what he earned last year before you'd known him for half an hour, but not what he paid taxes on — unless, of course, he saw you "understood" that kind of thing.

"It isn't that we don't think this is *nice*," another father said. "It *is*. What Mr. . . . uh, this *gentleman* is saying is that . . . well, it isn't *real*."

Not knowing that a silent scream had just rung out inside Maria's head, he smiled — to show he was a *real* nice man. He owned a number of dry cleaning shops, and he insisted that his help be every bit as nice as he was. People would be so impressed by that, they'd overlook the small mistakes you made while working on their clothes, he thought.

"Like it or not, the world out there" — he gestured vaguely toward the north, thinking that was where he'd driven over from; in fact, in that direction was the San Wakhaki Range, a wilderness — "the world of people and careers, is dog-eat-dog. There's only room for just so many *any*things. Up here, a person can lose sight of basic, fundamental truths like that, get out of touch with this old world you're going to have to deal with, sometime. You know what happens when an ath-a-lete gets out of shape." He smiled again. "He loses sharpness, his reaction time goes flooey. He can't compete successfully no more."

It had been a super dinner. Willa and her helpers really had excelled, spreading out a candle-lit buffet that from the Belgian Beef Stew and the Cold Lemon Chicken, through the Fettucine with Pesto and the Swiss Potato Gratin, to the Peach Cobbler, Pecan Pie, and Bittersweet Chocolate Cake was pure deliciousness, a whole lot better than the guests' last run of meals, even other ones they'd "eaten out." The kids' hope was that after such a meal their parents wouldn't have the heart, or energy, to criticize; they'd planned an after-dinner free exchange of thoughts, impressions, and ideas — this "Forum," as they called it.

In fact, the entire day's schedule had been constructed with an eye toward accentuating the positive. Shortly after their arrival, the parents had been given lunch — good, but not as great as dinner (quite on purpose), more sort of finger-lickin' food. Then, the visitors could — were urged to — wander, all around the town and totally unsupervised; nothing was off-bounds to them. The residents felt sure that parents would be pleased to see how neat and clean the rooms all were, and relieved to notice all of them were clearly *single* spaces — no round beds and big ol' mirrors anywhere. ("And naturally, they'll *all* believe it *always* looks this nice," said Roger at a planning meeting. People told him to shut up, of course — as usual. But once they'd gotten used to Rog, they couldn't help but like the guy.)

Also, up and down the main street, certain kids flew hugely colorful, enormous, homemade kites. Each kite's tail was made of black or Day-Glo letters forming somewhat enigmatic sentences, such as, "My Knows Is Growing," "Ear We Are, Together," and "March Time In The Key of See."

During their free-wander time, parents could also check out all the interesting and practical learning experiences their offspring were providing for each other, in such diverse fields as auto mechanics, carpentry, computers, cooking, electronics, gardening, and fitness. Not to mention music, naturally. Maria spent the time in some discomfort, taking Sookie's place and telling parents all about the different jobs —

careers — "they'd" done some research on. She also kept on wishing she could open up the parents' heads, and pour in kettlefuls of other kinds of townliness, some fuller explanations of the kites. Like telling them about the feeling that the kids all got — well, *almost* all of them — from being totally in charge of their commitments, from knowing that the things they thought and said, and tried out on one another, would not (importantly) be held against them. From having time to dream, to think, hang out, experiment, and not feel guilty. From (this is a peculiar one) feeling themselves grow up by reason of the potent interactions they were having, as with Omar, and the parents here today and most of all each other, interactions during which they dared to see themselves as non-dependent *equals*.

("I've got a *great* idea for when the parents are just circulating," Roger'd said, again, while plans were being made. "Why don't all of us who are keeping journals up here just put them in a pile someplace and let the parents just sort of *browse on through* our deepest fears and hopes and fantasies. Then, when they have heart attacks, we run and give them CPR and save their *lives*! Which puts them in our debt, of course, just like that lion with the whatsis in his foot, and means — " They cut him off, again.)

In the late afternoon, The Guise gave an unpretentious little concert on the porch (rich with Golden Oldies), while at the same time games of all-have-fun-together volleyball took place, and Babe presided over a nature walk (and mushroom tasting) for those with a bucolic turn of mind. Dinner was at seven-thirty, to be followed by the aforementioned "Forum," a time (as Roger said) when parents could stand up and testify how *perfect* everything (and -body) was, and how they wished that *they'd* had this same opportunity when *they* were seventeen, to take some time to find themselves, et cetera.

The Forum hadn't quite gone that-a-way, although at first there were some heartfelt compliments and gratitudes expressed. E-Man's father had predictably got up and done his *"most* constructive interactions" bit, and Sis and Mimimi's two moms had both expressed delight with how well organized and *punctual* the day's events had been, how positive and healthy everybody looked. Sis also spoke of the intangibles (important and available to people of her gender), telling everyone the place "felt right" to her, the moment she drove into town.

In fact, the first attack on what was going on up there had also started with a compliment, this one on the cooking, offered by a father in a dark blue linen blazer and an ascot, who owned a most successful dress shop, back in town.

"What bothers me a little, though," this man looked pained to say, "is that you people here are living what I'd have to label almost carefree lives, again. Or *still,* I guess you could say. Avoiding all responsibility. Just the way you used to do — my daughter's heard me say this once or twice — in high school."

Apparently, the third time was too much for that same daughter. Her name was Lisa, contrabassoonist with The Guise.

"But Daddy, can't you see the differences? This is mine, my choice," she said, "And I'm responsible

132

for me in ways I never was in high school. I'm working harder now than any time in my entire life, and *loving* it. Doesn't all that count for *something*?"

"And doesn't it also matter," added Parmenter, "that all of us are learning to cooperate and live as a community, and take, like, total care of our environment? Not just a room or an apartment, man, but an entire town?"

That was when the electrical contractor threw in his bit about what America was built on, and the dry cleaning guy sang backup with the dog-eat-dog material.

Seppy'd gotten to his feet to answer that one.

"I think we all remember what it's like back there, all right," he said. "And I think we all know we're going to have to compete, whether we like it or not. People are going to look at whatever it is I do, and they're going to compare it with somebody else's stuff. But that's okay with me; that just seems sensible. Hell, I like to have a choice myself. The thing that I don't like's that rhetoric you used. Frankly, I don't plan to either *be* a dog *or* eat one."

There was some scattered clapping. Not a big ovation, just a fast, nonverbal "yeah."

The dry cleaner wasn't about to let that pass, of course — not a guy who could communicate like him.

"Me neither," he said firmly, smiling still. You could tell he saw himself as moderate and sensible, a voice of reason and experience. A reservoir of information and of great good humor, a sort of human *Reader's Digest.* "Though some of my best friends are also *man's* best friends." He laughed, and so did people in his audience. "No, all I meant was that it's a mistake to let yourself become so easygoing — trusting — that some other guy with . . . well, a different *attitude* (let's say) can come along and take the shirt right off your back. Even if he then brings it to one of my places to get cleaned, I wouldn't want to see that happen." He scored another laugh. "And it just seems to me that living in a town like this is going to bring a person's guard down some. Cause him to relax. Maybe it's that pecan pie, but *I* feel lazier already!"

"Hell, why not call a spade a spade; a place like this'll make you *soft*," the electrical contractor said. "It has to. Up here there isn't any pressure. It's like being on vacation. Everything is 'mellow,' 'groovy,' right? I know the words you use." He chuckled at his wisdom. "Well, forget about it. By the time that you kids leave this place, you'll need a halfway house to *re*-compress in. Get a little hard again." (Roger's eyebrows did a number.) "I doubt that some of you could even handle *college*, as you are right now. If you went up against some kids with *drive*, I think they'd leave you in the dust, no kidding."

"Just out of weirdness," piped up Boid, "where do you stand on the comprehensive nuclear test ban issue?"

The contractor swiveled right around to look at him. He wanted to be sure which kid it was, in case he ever found him in his house, or lying in the street somewhere.

"Hundred percent against," he said. "The Russians always find a way to cheat. There's no such thing as verifiable. Take my word for it."

"But. . .," started several voices from around the

134

room, including E-Man's father, Jake's mother, and both of Seppy's parents. A woman's voice cut through them all, however.

"Before we get *completely* off the subject," she began, "which I *believe* is this town and how it may affect our sons and daughters, I'd like to raise another issue." She touched her hair and took a breath. "People that I know, my friends and neighbors who know Sophie, they're asking me a lot of *different* sorts of questions: Who's responsible for all those kids up there? Who's going to see they don't run wild? How can you have a moment's peace, knowing she might be talked into using drugs, or God knows what-all?"

"Oh, *Mom*," said Sophie. She was the one with the crazy frosted hairdo that Maria liked so much. "We've gone through this a hundred times already. I told you just this afternoon that I and all the people here — "

"No, I'm sorry, Sophie." Having overcome the test ban group, she wasn't about to be shouted down by her own daughter. "I want to hear what *other* people have to say. Like, other *parents*."

There was a sort of babble for a moment, a babble the contractor didn't join. He'd needed only one quick look at Sophie. That mother was *at least* two years and skatey-seven tricks too late. If the kid had worn a sign it couldn't have been clearer. He turned and gave his wife a wink.

"We've felt the same concerns, of course," the dress-shop man began. "I, perhaps, more strongly than my wife. *She* believes — "

"*She* believes it's completely a matter of trust, the same as it was at home," the woman right beside

135

him said, in no mood to be spoken for, apparently. "Most of the same friends that Lisa saw at home are up here now. She's seventeen. We can't make her decisions for her. She's heard what we think since the age of nothing; she's either bought it or she hasn't. And, frankly, my opinion is her friends would be more apt to help her if she needed help than . . . get her into trouble of some sort."

Lisa's friends — the band and the others — naturally applauded.

"That's all very well to *think*," the other mother said. "And we trust Sophie, too — "

" — *sometimes*," her husband said, and certain people laughed.

" — but still you've got your public opinion to consider," his wife went on. "Your younger children hear . . . like, this and that that's said about their sister. People pass remarks to *you*. They aren't satisfied with trust. What other people do is they suspect the worst, and frankly I don't blame them. With all the stories in the paper every day. . . ."

"I'd like to make a comment here," said Omar, standing up, resplendent in his uniform, gold star and all. "I happen to be sheriff of this county — Hupee County, just in case you're not all that familiar with the territory — and so, in certain ways, I have the same concerns that many of you parents do. Illegal drugs, as everybody knows, are now a major law enforcement problem, and so I took it as my duty. . . ."

And so, away he went, telling them a lot about his training and experience, making himself sound like a cross between a physician specializing in the treatment of kids turned on by every kind of dope imaginable (and who thus had every symptom at his fingertips), and one of those sniffing dogs you see in buses, outside planes, and in the holds of ships, sometimes. In sum, he said that he believed Mariasburg was squeaky-clean, and from what he'd seen of the kids (on numerous unexpected visits at all hours of the day and night), they were much too smart and well brought up to . . . on and on, you get the picture.

Omar's remarks were pretty potent stuff though, thought Maria. She could definitely imagine some of the parents, like Sophie's mother, telling her friends that *The Sheriff of Hupee County* was such a constant presence in the town that it was almost like having Arnold Schwarzenegger up there — someone *good* the kids not only welcomed but, like, *idolized*, almost, having nothing in the world to hide. And Maria was quite right.

"That's very interesting, and comforting," said Sophie's mother, just as soon as he had finished. And she smiled. "I appreciate your interest in our children, Sheriff."

Maria shot a look at Mimimi, Sophie one at Lisa, Etta one at Wendy, Willa one at Noralee, and on and on and on. Everybody chewed the insides of their mouths in unison. His "interest in their children" — what a line!

"Let me ask just two more questions," the contractor said. "Just to satisfy my curiosity. How many of you parents actually believe — sheriff or no sheriff and appearances to the contrary — that there hasn't been a single case of drugs or alcohol consumed, or other kinds of hanky-panky going on up here? I'm sure you take my meaning. Now, would you raise your hands on that, just parents, please?"

Some parents smiled, looked down, or shook their heads (perhaps in great disgust), but no one raised a hand.

"Well, so much for the really healthy atmosphere up here," the father said. "And now my other question. How many believe their *own* kids are, or soon will be, involved in such activities?"

He put his own hand up this time, and was joined by two other fathers, both of boys, both now smiling broadly.

"Well," he said again, "I'm glad to see two other total realists, at least. And as for all you kids, nice going. Meaning no offense, but your folks are just as dumb as you have always thought they were."

He threw a chuckle out into the silence of the room, showing (so he thought) that what he'd said was only good clean fun.

"Nice going, sir, yourself," Maria said, getting to her feet and smiling on her own account. Seppy closed his eyes; he knew that smile.

"Meaning even less offense than you did, *but*," she said, "you are just as full of shit as not just your own son, but Mister Rogers, Roy, and Trigger said you were. But wait." She held a finger up. "You could be right on one thing, though. I know if *I* belonged to you, I'd need some drinks to help me to forget it. Meaning no offense, of course." She sat back down.

Sis clapped delightedly and laughed out loud. So did certain other parents who weren't about to sit completely still and be called dumb by a fat blowhard who (some of them remembered) had used to

138

copy everybody's lab notes. A lot of kids stamped feet and whistled; Omar got a twinkle in his eyes; the heavyset contractor's face began to glow.

Maria got back up. But now she skipped across the room to stand by the contractor's place. She wanted to look loopy. She was smiling once again, but differently.

"Just kidding — silly me!" she said. "Younger generation humor — hear a joke, you try to make a bigger one; I guess we're too competitive sometimes. I hope you're not at all offended, really; your son thinks you're the greatest. Everybody up here's heard him say that, lots of times." She swirled a finger round and round behind her back, and quite a few kids clapped. "What I *really* meant to say was: if my mother's dumb . . . well, pass the dumb. 'Cause what she understands is sets — set theory, right? Math class, back in school? My mother knows my growing-up set isn't anything at all like hers. The two of us grew up with different teachers, different friends, and . . . well," she paused and then went on, but now at breakneck speed, "with different looks, and houses, weapons, clothes, an' presidents (God knows), *and* birth control devices (that's for sure), and music, and deodorants, I guess. Not to mention different genes." She slowed back down again. "Well, given all those differences, would she be smart if she believed she'd know how I would think and act in every situation? Or what my needs are, all the time? Well, she doesn't, so she must be smart, all right?" She stood there, looking down at him, still totally relaxed and friendly.

The electrical contractor's face had paled a little,

but was still quite red. Maria was a first for him; he wondered if she *could* be crazy. What was all that stuff about deodorants?

"My son won't think and act like me in every situation, either." He said that sentence slowly, looking straight ahead, then gave his head a quarter turn, to look up at Maria. "But let me tell you this, young lady. He had better watch those needs of his and be real careful just what lines he chooses to get out of. I didn't mean to say your mother's stupid; she can keep on reading Doctor Spock and let you do whatever with your life. But there are also lots of guys like me who still decide what happens in our homes, and with our kids. And kids like you had better not forget it."

He turned away and sipped his coffee then (though there was just a swallow in his cup and it was cold). He thought he'd been a real good sport, considering. The room was silent. Maria stood there for a moment, shrugged, and went back to her seat.

E-Man's father jumped right up and made a little curtain-closing speech in which he thanked and complimented everyone for what he termed "a frank and useful sharing of opinions and awarenesses." He said that he was confident that everybody there agreed the town was "bold, creative, answering a need." Though still "too young a project to be judged," it did (he felt) show ample promise. Therefore, then, he gave the town his blessing and endorsed his son's involvement in "a most worthwhile experiment."

After he stopped speaking, there was general applause, and with a lot of people standing up and talking, too, it really wasn't possible to judge how many people *hadn't* clapped (if any), and were, in fact, tight-lipped and looking angry. Willa, from the kitchen door, saw the E-Man's father go shake hands with the electrical contractor, throw an arm around his shoulder, get the guy involved in (seeming) friendly conversation. Sis came and hugged Maria and then, perhaps reflexively, started cleaning tables with her.

A lot of other mothers, and some fathers, too, got into helping straighten up. Few people even noticed, later on, that the contractor stopped the sheriff on the porch when he was leaving, and jotted down an answer that he got from him.

17

Sore Loser

RELCO, Inc.
Electrical Contractors
Box 138
Cinverguenza, QA 0007-35810

Mr. George L—
Hupee County Clerk
Hupee City, QA

Dear Mr. L—,

Recently, having lost our way on some small, unmarked back roads, my wife and I found ourselves in a tiny town in Hupee County that calls itself "Mariasburg." My understanding is that perhaps its legal name is Jacks R Better.

My wife and I were pretty much surprised to find that almost every person living in the town was aged eighteen or under, and that these young people seemed, in effect, to be operating some sort of a semieducational institution there, financed by one of their own number.

I'm no expert on either state law or county regulations but it seems likely to me that the residents of this town are almost certainly violating quite a number of each, due to their ages, life-style, and lack of formal government (charter, zoning, etc.), as well as operating an unlicensed and/or unregistered school and other businesses.

As you'll notice, I'm sending a copy of this letter to the office of Governor Palattice (who I had the privilege of supporting very strongly in the last election) in the hope that the County and the State authorities will take appropriate action in a case like this. Although for obvious reasons (such as the possibility of violent, vengeful action on their part) I'd prefer that the town residents not know of my interest in this matter, I'd appreciate hearing from you as to any actions taken by the county and the state and any resolutions reached.

> Very truly yours,
> Hobart B. R—, President

cc Gov. J.P. Palattice

18

Travel Talk

After the Open House, Mariasburg relaxed. You could tell that from the noise at feeding times, the jokes, the clothes that people wore (or almost didn't wear, or wore together), and the music that was played. The great thing that had hapened was that not one single parent, packing up the car, day after, had stuffed a kid in there beside the Samsonites, and driven him/her home.

Surprise, surprise; relief, relief. Roger found an unexpected thirty bucks (two tens, a two, and an eight, he said) inside some zippered hiding place and blew it on a Dogs-Eat-Dogs Soirée. Menu: chicken franks and Kool-Aid, with taco chips and Twinkies. Entertainment: climbing the rungless ladder of success (two poles — peeled aspens, green — set side by side about a foot apart and smeared with axle grease), and games of Capture the Shirt (right off the other person's back).

Omar's stock was at a high, of course. That speech — what taste, what understanding he had showed; his description of their characters, their charm, their girlish/boyish *incorruptibility* had been, no question, proof of his perception and intelligence. Sophie told him that her mom said he was "cute." Omar acted pleased but raged inside. That bag. Did she think a guy like him had time for older women?

Maria felt a whole lot more relieved than anyone. She'd been afraid she'd shorted out the electrician's son, although he'd told her not to worry ("he's much more full of shit than what you said"). It seemed as if her two volcanic problems, Omar and the parents, were . . . she wouldn't dare say *solved*, but, well, *inactive* for the moment. And though her thoughts of Sookie gave her sadness-stabs, she made herself feel better with a mental fortune cookie: *Like cucumbers, old friends keep coming back.* Maybe in a month or so, if she went down to visit Sis, she'd kind of ask around. No one at the town blamed Sookie. Let's hear it for *The Prodigal Daughter*, this one time.

She hadn't given any thought to The Defenders of the Fate. Not that she expected they would go away if she ignored them. She'd simply been too busy for the past ten days. And, too, because she'd never seen them, they were more forgettable; possibly this Sledge would just move on to other interests, get a job. As long as Omar stayed away from her and kept on hangin' with "the guys," she didn't have to think of either him *or* those Defenders.

But suddenly, one day, he didn't and she did.

She'd been doing dinner dishes, gotten really hot, so she'd gone back to her room to swap the sweatshirt she'd been wearing for a tank top. She'd taken off the shirt and dug the top out of her clothing

145

chest. Naked to the waist, she'd turned back toward the door and ducked her head into the top, wiggled it on down below her breasts. Her head came up to shake her hair back into place, and there was Omar, standing in the doorway.

Chill.

She couldn't tell, of course, how long he'd been there, but his little simper-smile gave her a clue; like, plainly, long enough. Maria was real glad she had a tan and — anyway — was not the blushing type.

"Didn't mean to make you jump," he said. She wondered if she had; she hoped not. "I hollered from across the road when you came out of dinner, but you couldn't hear, I guess. So I just trailed you over. I've got a thing to tell you." He made a little mouth. "Not great news, but maybe not *too* terrible. Sledge called again. He says he'd like to see you up at his place, sometime soon. Although he said he'd come down here if you 'obliged him to.' That's the way he put it."

Maria matched the face he'd made.

"Me?" she said. "Why me? Why is it always *me* fanatics want to see? I think I must remind them of their mothers. Or possibly the prophet Ruth. Was she a prophet? Yes, I think she must have been. She wasn't any total loss, I know that much."

Omar didn't play along. "He said he had to see the one they named the town for. I guess it's obvious," he said, and smiled. "He thinks you run things here."

"But that's a crock," Maria said. "Couldn't you have told him I'm the village joke? Or got closest

146

to the stake when we played Name That Town croquet?"

"I could have, I suppose," the sheriff said. "But what I thought was: Hell, why bother? The best thing you can do with guys like him, from a psychological point of view, is never rock the boat when you don't have to. The less you tell them 'No,' the less they're apt to have their little tantrums. Why have the guy come down and start some sort of hubbub here? I mean, if worst came to the worst, we could handle it all right, but probably one of my deputies'd say something in town, and it'd get into the papers. . . ."

"Great. That's all we need," Maria said. "A spot on *The Today Show*." She started chewing on the inside of her mouth again, but caught herself before she'd taken more than one good chomp.

"Okay," she said, thinking *what the hell*. "Why not? I'll go up there. Just don't say I have to wear a bonnet, or a veil."

Omar laughed. "Sledge *is* a little sexist," he admitted. "By contemporary standards." Maria thought that sounded slightly strange. "Of course," the sheriff said, "he'd say that how he treats the women is *God's* will. Not something *he* decided on."

"Fine," Maria said, "just lovely. Don't blame him, he was only following orders, right? That's great. Now, when and how — "

"As far as getting there," Omar continued, "I thought it might make sense if you went up with me. Just like we talked about. It's possible he might be . . . well, a little *calmer*, if I'm there." He pulled an earlobe. "You see, it just so happens that the

County Sheriff — me — is the highest civil officer that Sledge and all his folks accept. You know, as far as having any say-so over them."

Maria didn't need much time to think it over. Omar was a dick-head, sure enough. But if she was going to get herself called . . . what? a "Satan pedermaster," or some other folksy little put-down, it wouldn't feel bad to have a dick-head with a gun and some authority, on hand.

"Okay," she said again. "I'd like to have the company. Just tell me when you want to go. And maybe, going up, you can fill me in some more on Sledge and his *paisanos*."

"Um," said Omar, noncommittally. "Well, how about, say, Thursday, then? I could pick you up at ten, if that's okay."

"Just great," Maria said.

He nodded, turned toward the door, and started leaving.

"And Sheriff," called Maria, sharply. He turned, his body swung around before his face was ready, maybe. He had one look on at the moment that he turned, and then another look took over. The first one went with lotteries and jackpots, dressing rooms right after Super Bowls, Maria thought. The other one was much more . . . *normal*, for the circumstances.

"What?" he said. "What is it?"

"Nothing, really — or, just, thanks for going up with me," she said and smiled at him, ignoring the disturbance in her chest.

Seppy didn't take it well at all, the news that she was going up to Sledge's place with Omar. He'd come on by her room on Wednesday night, and after he'd expressed surprised delight at finding her at home, he'd put both hands together and made a comic dive onto her bed. There, he sort of wiggle-waddled on his elbows and his knees, his butt up in the air.

"Yes, here's the big old horseshoe crab," he said. "He's burrowed in the sand. And wishing there was someone he could play with, so he wouldn't feel so crabby."

Maria smiled, but felt a little stab of pain, a little pang. The one thing that the town had cost — was costing — her was Seppy-time, the hunks of privacy that they were used to having.

She draped herself on top of him, maneuvered so's to blow into his ear.

"Here comes a young crabette, with horseshoes on her mind," she crooned. "This is called a 'leaner,' and a score of three for her."

"Flip us over on our back and we are helpless," Seppy said, holding onto her and rolling over, her on top of him. "See? Our claws still work" — he pincered her, she squealed — "but otherwise we can't resist . . . well, anything. Especially temptation. In fact, what I came by to ask — suggest — is maybe you and I could pack a lunch and hike it up to Roger's waterfall tomorrow. That one he found up near the ridge? Then you could put me on my back for *hours*, without the slightest chance of suitemates coming in, or anything. You could be the horseshoe, I could be — "

Maria made a yucky face and he shut up.

"Damn!" she said. "I can't. But raincheck me, okay? Tomorrow's just a total washout. I'll tell you what. We'll play a doubleheader Friday, how would that be? Lunch and dinner and then camp out for the night. Okay? The thing about tomorrow is. . . ." And then she told him what she'd planned, arranged, to do.

"What?" he said. He took her shoulders, pushed them like a barbell being bench-pressed, and sat up. "You're nuts. You can't do that."

She didn't like his language but, considering the provocation, she only put her eyebrows up.

"That's absolutely crazy," Seppy said again. "Going *anywhere* alone with Omar, number one. And 'specially to Sledge's, for God's sake. Those weirdos always seem to be a woman short, trying to find their son a wife, or something. I'm not kidding. You could end up chained down in a cellar hole, until you learned to treat somebody 'nice.' You really can't go up there, Mya. It isn't worth the chance that you'd be taking. Or chan*ces*, counting Omar."

"Well, I'm going, Sep," Maria said. "It seems to me this could be real important for the town. I grant you it's a little . . . risky, but I'm going to do it anyway." She tried to lighten up. "It's like the kid said in that movie *Risky Business*? Sometimes you just have to say it. I'm betting Omar's telling me the truth this time." She cocked her head and smiled.

Seppy wasn't buying light. At all. He grumped up to his feet, mumbling some lines about "contorted values," "martyrs," "disregard for people's *somethings*."

Maria tried to get him to sit down again and try to understand, but he said he believed he understood too well already. It was a simple matter of priorities, he said.

"I guess I'm really not *surprised*," he said. "Just real, real sorry."

He shook his head, and pecked her on the cheek, and wandered out the door.

"How about that Friday deal?" she called out after him.

"We'll see," came drifting back to her.

Omar came not in the Jeep but in his squad car, once again in uniform. Clearly, they were on official business. She slithered in beside him, which put the riot gun between them, up there on the dash in brackets, and the metal grille behind her head. This girl is riding shotgun, that's for sure (she thought).

"They all think he's a prophet," Omar said, when they were on the highway. "The latest in a line that stretches back to all the famous ones. Moses and the gang. He goes along with that." He gave a little laugh. "In fact, he gave them the idea."

"He must be real persuasive," said Maria. "But it still amazes me, the way these guys can do it. Supposin' someone said to you: 'Hey, man. I just now got the word from God. He said we all should grab a gun and warm the tractors up — get ready to plow ass.' What's your first reaction? You wouldn't get your Ray-Bans on and jump on the John Deere. Come *on*. You'd make the guy a reservation at the nearest rubber room. You'd try to get him off the streets."

"Well, sure," said Omar. "Chances are I would, in lots of cases. I'd beware of them false prophets, like the Bible says. But like with Sledge, or — well, you've heard of Manson, right? — sometimes a guy's got something kind of . . . magical, almost, and it just rings some sort of bell with people, even if it's sort of crazy, too. Maybe he says things you've kind of thought yourself, for years, but never heard put into just those words, before." He tapped Maria on the knee. "God works in wondrous ways," he said. "That's in the Bible, too, you know. And look — just for the sake of argument — why shouldn't God talk to someone in our country, even in this county, here? That's all the old-time prophets were, just guys. From one real little area, much smaller than this state. Of course" — he waved a hand — "I grant you Sledge takes some things to extremes. Like, in certain ways, it's almost like he thinks *he's* God." He shook his head. "To give you one example: he owns *everything* up there, not just the ranch and the equipment but every other thing that anybody has, right down to their socks and underwear. He acts as God's custodian, he says." He shook his head again. "All the other folks, his family and all, have nothing."

Maria chewed on that a while, looking out the window. *She* had on some very blah gray socks and rather brief red briefs with this word "vigilance" across the back of them, in black. The underwear belonged to her, but she had borrowed socks from Mimimi. She was also wearing blue jeans, not a real tight pair, and a big, baggy plaid shirt over a big, baggy gray t-shirt. Her hair was in a braid, wrapped with a plain brown rubber band, and she had no makeup on or adornments, even earrings. She'd thought of putting on a dress, but that seemed *too* accommodating. Also, maybe, dangerous and provocative: all her summer dresses showed a fair amount of skin.

"How come he doesn't recognize, like, state or federal authority?' she said, at last. "What's his problem, with that?"

Omar gave an offhand little chuckle.

"Atheistic Jewish communists," he said. "He thinks they run the country. The same ones that control the papers and TV. And the movies and the banks, and Wall Street, naturally. He can reel the names right off. You'd recognize a lot of them. They call the tunes, he says, and the Congress and the courts and governors all dance. He's got it figured that — I think — like, eighteen cents of every dollar that a person pays in taxes goes to them, or Israel. He says that they control the schools, too — that this secular humanism you hear about them teaching is nothing more than atheistic Jewish communism, just like they have on the kibbutzes, over there."

"Good lord," Maria said. "He's one of *those*? A fascist, hate-ist, sickoid? I thought that he was strictly like, 'Repent, you sinners, for the world is going to end a week from Tuesday.' One of *that* kind, like a comic strip, almost — the guys in sheets and beards, with signs."

"Well, he believes in Armageddon, sure enough," the sheriff said, and smiled. "The world's last battle, taking place in good ol' Hupee County, as well as lots of other places. But what he wants to figure out ahead of time, I guess, is who is who, exactly, in the neighborhood. Where does everybody stand on, like, the major issues. That way, when the shooting starts, he'll know exactly when his ass needs covering. You've got to give him credit, in a

153

way. Everything he does ties in with his beliefs; he's got a pretty complex world reduced to simple terms. Actually, once you accept his basic premises, it looks as if the guy could possibly be right."

Omar kept on grinning broadly while he said that last part, and Maria had a sense that she was being jerked around, put on, big O'd. Could be that this was Omar's way of getting even, being the great master of psychology, playing little mind games with her. She told herself she didn't have a thing to be afraid of. Everybody in the town had seen her leave with him, and knew exactly where they planned to go. Well, maybe not exactly. Only Omar knew *exactly*.

And fifteen minutes after that, he turned onto a rutted road that disappeared into the woods, real fast. There weren't any markings on it, only signs — clearly not the works of Elks, or the Kiwanis. Maria found their style to be uncomfortably familiar: "Very Privat Road," "NO Salesmen or Blasfemers," "We Don forgive You Trespassers."

They went up it for a half a mile or so, going in a lower gear and bouncing some, with woods on either side. But then, quite suddenly — surprisingly — they came out of all the trees and onto open ground. Ahead of them was mostly planted fields and pasture land, a hilltop with a massive house and tin-roofed barns on it. And all around that area, there was a chain-link fence, with a large steel gate in it, behind which was a little fieldstone structure, not much bigger than an outhouse.

Omar honked — two shorts and a long. A boy came out of the little house, a sort of lanky, puppy-looking boy: dark blond hair in a Prince Valiant cut, a round and open face with freckles, and a lot of big white teeth. He was wearing floppy, home-made-looking clothes. Maria would have said he was about fourteen, although in one respect he looked much older. That was the weapon that he carried with indifferent ease, dangling from one big paw: a Rambo/A-Team kind of gun, the sort that made a lot of holes in anything, in very little time.

The sheriff said, "Hi, Japh," as he unlocked the gate. The boy did not reply, but touched his cap bill to Maria as he looked away from her. She thought he might be blushing. When they had gone on through the gate and were headed for the big stone house atop the hill, Omar said the boy was Japhet, one of Sledge's seven sons. He'd also sired seven daughters, Omar said, but being "basically an easygoing guy," he'd spread "the work" between four different women, one of whom had "gone away." The other three were still in residence, along with all the kids and Sledge's "hired men"; two fellows Omar said he found "a bit peculiar, certain ways."

Maria said she couldn't wait to meet them, them and all the family. "And by the way," she said, "is 'Sledge' his first or last name? Short for 'Sledginald,' or something? I've been wondering."

Omar said he didn't really know for sure, but that, one time, he'd heard a story.

"This fella said that years ago, he'd gone to prison. Sledge had, way down south someplace. Maybe he'd been preaching what he practiced, or doing miracles without a license — some little thing, this fella didn't say. But anyway, this was some backwoods county prison farm down there, where everybody did hard time, and naturally it had its pecking order in amongst the convicts. In the real big penitentiaries, King Con is apt to be an older guy with dough and power on the outside, like a 'boss," but in these smaller jails you beat your way up to the top. Beat, cut, stomp — whatever. So, first day on the rock pile, Sledge — just plain old Joe-or-Jim-or-Pete back then and nothing but a kid — he gets the word about who's who and what's expected of a 'new boy,' such as him, starting that same night. I guess you can imagine." Omar grinned. "But he says 'Hey, no way,' I guess, and loud enough so that the Big Guy hears. And then he adds some commentary. Apparently quite personal and pointed and nothing anyone could possibly mistake for flattery. Of course the Big Guy starts right after him; he's going to pound him into paste right then and there. He knows the screws won't stop it; as far as they're concerned, that's entertainment. But Pete-or-Jim-or-Joe don't wait for this to happen, according to the story. He takes his big old hammer in both hands — the thing'd have a ten- or twelve-pound head on it — and slings it right across the rock pile at this guy. And this is the amazing part — a 'miracle,' this fella said — it hits him right between the eyes and drops him in his tracks." Omar made a fist and hit the steering wheel for emphasis. "Stone dead, of course."

Omar smiled. "At some other institution they'd have named him 'David,' probably. And given him some extra time to serve," he said. "But the inmates of that place were less . . . *allusive*, and the warden didn't care if there was one less mouth to feed. In any case, they simply called him 'Sledge' and that was it. I guess he must have liked the name all right, to bring it all the way up here with him."

"Um," Maria said. They'd reached the house.

19

Sledge

"I hope you understand now, Miss Maria. I hope you hear my words not only through your ears but through your heart as well. There won't be any Switzerlands: no neutrals, no one on the sidelines. Once it starts, you're either with us or against us. On the side of righteousness or lost forever."

And Sledge had smiled and raised his eyebrows, showed her one clean there-you-have-it palm. He had a gentle, urgent voice, not ignorant but hardly professorial, more like a salesman's voice, a *carpet* salesman, possibly, a true believer in the need for wall-to-wall, throughout.

There was no way that Maria was prepared for him, this Sledge. She was sure the sheriff must have been real close to wetting pants — the bastard — waiting for the moment she first met the guy. Or maybe not; who knows? In any case, she thought she hadn't even blinked. It took an effort but she was pretty sure she hadn't.

Add up all the facts she had: one, her dream (that "Satan pedermaster" night), two, the name of Sledge (and how he'd come by it), and three, what everybody *knew* about fanatics . . . add those and you got, like what? A wild-eyed screamer — right? — huge (or anyway, real tall), with long, unkempt black hair and beard. *Of course?* Don't be ridiculous!

This guy was small, soft-spoken, light-eyed; his skin was smooth, but had a mellow tan; he wasn't in the least bit *weathered.* Judging from the age of his children, he had to be . . . oh, forty, *anyway,* but he looked younger. Even after he took off his floppy cap and showed her that his honey-colored head was mostly bald on top and that the remaining hair up there was fine, and kind of grayish blond. His baldness, in a way, just added to his *cuteness* (so Maria thought), put "kewpie doll" into her mind, on top of "boyish" and "appealing."

He'd met them at the front door of the house — Maria saw how thick the walls were — and had taken them at once into the kitchen, so that she could meet "the family." They all were seated, eating, at two trestle tables, huge ones, side by side. It was the biggest kitchen that Maria'd ever seen, even bigger than the World-of-Willa, back there at the 'burg.

Sledge said, "This is Miss Maria, from up at Jacks-'r-better."

Then he gave the names of everyone at both the tables, starting with the older men (called Josh and Enos), each presiding at the head of one of them. Those two looked *perfect* for Defenders of the Fate, Maria thought. The Josh was lean and bearded, wearing overalls; he had the wildest bushy eyebrows up above the oddest loopy eyes she'd ever seen. The Enos one was almost neckless, bald and squat with these enormous upper arms, stretching out the sleevelets of his khaki t-shirt; his pants were made of camouflage material. He had about a two-day beard, divided on one jawbone by a jagged pink and white canal, the scar of some great cut that never had been stitched, apparently. Though Josh had simply nodded at Maria, this one said some words to her. Well, *sort of* words. What it sounded like to her was gibberish, just nonsense syllables, but still she answered him politely with, "Hello, I'm pleased to meet you."

The women and most all the younger people (certainly the boys) just barely looked at her, bringing up their eyes as Sledge pronounced their names, but dropping them again right afterwards, as if they didn't want to stay in touch with her too long. The biggest boys were fully grown and older than she was, Maria thought. All three of them were sizable, clearly taller than their father, but they'd inherited his soft, light eyes and that same smooth and round-faced youthfulness. Give them different clothes and haircuts and all of Sledge's kids except the youngest ones — a pair of eight- or nine-year-olds — could pass for surfers, rather than . . . whatever you would call them now. "Fanatics" wouldn't work, Maria thought; a lot of surfers were fanatics, too.

Maria thought the girls were beautiful. Tense — and spooky-looking, sure — but beautiful. They and all three women wore long dresses and all of them had outdoor looks and pretty much their father's/husband's coloring. The girl whose chair was closest to the place Maria stood seemed about her age and so, before she'd even thought what she was doing, Maria offered her a hand when Sledge called out her name, Naomi. The girl ignored it for a blink or two, but then reached out and gave it one quick pump and (unlike all the others) maybe looked a little pleased. Maria thought the younger children shot quick looks at Sledge when she did that, but if he changed expression, she had been too late to catch him at it.

Omar wasn't introduced, and neither did he greet the people at the tables. Maria had the feeling he and everybody there were on familiar terms, though. The hired men (who he had said he found "a bit peculiar") seemed to her to make a point of looking anywhere but right at Omar. It was as if they held a grudge, or were afraid he'd do some really gross or shameless act, if they encouraged him at all. Or maybe they were overawed by his authority, Maria thought, if County Sheriff was the top man on the mortal, civic totem pole, to them.

With all the introductions over with, Sledge led them from the kitchen, down a hall, to what he called "our chapter room."

A creepy place, Maria thought, the moment she stepped into it.

What it made her think of, first, is what is called a "chapel" at an undertaker's. There was a little platform with a lectern on it. Behind the lectern were three armchairs, now rearranged by Sledge to make a little semicircle. That way, she and Omar could sit flanking him and faced in his direction. In front of them and (naturally) below the platform, there were three straight-backed benches, one behind the other — room for the entire "family" and more, Maria thought. The only other furniture in the room was another backless padded bench up on the platform, off to one side. There weren't any windows in the room, as far as you could tell; the walls were draped with heavy purple hangings, bordered with a shiny gold material. Some of them were partly pulled aside, looped back the way a window curtain is sometimes, and when Maria's eyes became accustomed to the dimness of the place, she saw that there were racks behind the hangings, racks containing weapons, tools, and other implements.

It was in this (most peculiar) setting Sledge began to tell her what was what. About such trivialities as final battles, and the last days of the world, and the fate of all mankind.

"It's by your fruits that I can get to know you, Miss Maria," Sledge was saying to her now. On his lap he held "The Special and Authentic Bible of the Militant Lord God." That was what he'd called it when he'd picked it up from off the lectern. He'd opened it and riffled through the pages, smiling down at it. Maria saw it looked just like a standard raise-your-hand-and-take-the-oath-type Bible, except that certain sections were inked over and that some other pages had been scissored out. Also, here and there some words or sentences were written in the margin, with arrows showing where they should be put into the text.

"When I learn about your town — the quality of life up there, the work and other pastimes of the people, the secrets of their hearts — well, then, I'll know. And when the moment, the inevitable comes. . . ." He paused and looked into an upper corner of the room, as if there was some information or a timepiece there, counting off the minutes and the hours and the days. ". . . and the explosions start, the clouds of living fire rage across the earth, imploding walls and vaporizing flesh, then we shall either march together, terrible in might and majesty, rapturous in spirit, or. . . ." He smiled; the palm came out again. ". . . *we*, the people here, along with other neighbors, *we* will march alone and send you screaming to the holocaustal pit of everlasting agony where temperatures of twenty thousand degrees centigrade are not all that uncommon."

Maria snuck a look at Omar, hoping she could get some clue from his expression. No such luck. Going by *his* face, Sledge might have said, "It's been a little warm for lima beans, this week."

"Now, Miss Maria," Sledge leaned slightly forward in his chair. "Do you and all the people in your town believe in one great lord, thy God, eternal, maker of the heavens and the earth?" He didn't scream that out or anything, just sounded interested, the way the carpet guy would be while asking, "Do you believe the front hall, here, will be a heavy traffic area?"

"Well, I don't know," Maria said. "Speaking for myself, I am a 'very much in favor' of the proposition or, in simple terms, a 'yes.' It's hard to put in words all I believe, but there is definitely God in it, a loving force and source, that's always been and always will be. I wouldn't want to speak for everybody else back there, but I know there are some people who believe about the same things I do."

She thought she'd try to be both honest and offhand; in the absence of a lot of help from Omar, that seemed like much the best idea. Maybe Sledge would think that she was just a pleasant, slightly flaky kid, living with a bunch of dittos. Then he could march off some other way on Armageddon day, having filed Mariasburg under "harmless": no threat whatever to God's plan, or even to that tender ass of his.

"But towns all have communal points of view," said Sledge, persisting. "Take the Sisters, for example. The Sisters (as they called themselves) of Sanity. *Their* town had a point of view, an evil Godless one, and rotten to the core."

Sledge rubbed his hands together and proceeded to explain that point of view in warm and colorful detail. Summarized, the explanation was that they had mated standard "kikeamerika" with something he called "dykeamerika" and that produced, as offspring, foul mutations such as feminism, pacifism, commune-ism, and the ERA (which, they were sure, would let them marry one another and get propaganda jobs, like teaching school).

Maria sat there, semistunned. Although the sheriff had served up a warning, fed her lines from Sledge's phrase book (such as "atheistic Jewish communists"), *she* had, basically, refused to swallow. It had been easier to think that maybe Omar was just trying to scare her, getting even. Now she had to face the fact that this guy Sledge was looney-tunes, and she was sitting in a house (with two-foot walls) with him, and only one lech/dick-head for protection.

"Because," Sledge said, "the Sisters were an evil tribe, which went against the laws of nature and of nature's God, the great Jehovah snuffed them out. He did it His way — for that time, at any rate — slowly, slowly, slowly. Stretching out their agony. We weren't in the neighborhood just then, of course, or He could have had it done in jig time, all at once, no waiting." He sighed, perhaps regretfully. "In any case, they had a point of view — as I was saying — and it proved to be not only flawed, but fatal. So now I need to know the one that your Mariasburg embraces. *Your* town, Miss Maria."

Maria shook her head.

"But I don't think we have one," she insisted. "It's just a place where kids can get their heads together."

"Just their heads?" Sledge said. "Not other parts, as well?"

For the first time, then, he moved *his* head and looked away from her to Omar, and then right back at her. By the time *she* looked at Omar, he was just as he had been before: totally impassive, the observer; too late again, Maria thought.

"I wouldn't know," she said, trying not to let the anger she was feeling tint her voice. "It seems to me that that'd be their private business."

"Really, now," said Sledge. "Their private business? Their teenaged *privates'* business is now private business, is it? Who cares what parents think, what God commands? Just leave it to the beaver, our young lady says. To me and all my fellow teens."

Now he shook *his* head. Maria thought: *uh-oh*. His eyes were getting wider, wilder, really not at all like those of someone (mainly) into broadloom, $18.95 a yard.

"This is the business of Beelzebub!" he cried, his flat hand cracking on the Bible's cover. " 'Private business,' 'freedom of choice' — the cant of all the humanists, and onanists, and satanists. The sodomite's delighted cry: 'Just let me choose!' Children —

164

and to me you are a child still, Miss Maria, for all your womanly . . . development — should be given only very simple choices; they have no *private* business, whatsoever. Not when we are talking cleanliness of mind and speech, of heart and body. Children in this house are taught such things — and manners and obedience — by me and by my surrogate. The only choice they have to make is that between the things we teach them and the rod."

He got up, walked across the room, and pulled the purple fabric back a little further. There on a rack were half a dozen switches, whippy-looking things like willow withes. He picked one up and brought it back and gave it to Maria.

"Imagine that across your bare backside a dozen times or more," he said. "That's just what our Naomi got last week — eh, Brother Omar? A little private business just between the two of them, that time, done in this very room." His bright eyes danced with pleasure. "Your friend the sheriff is the only other man I trust," he told Maria, "to do the right thing by young people. Give them what they need."

Maria sat there holding the round wooden rod and feeling the cold sweat trickle down her sides. '*Brother* Omar'? and 'the only other man I trust . . .'? Was this what she'd been brought there for? So he could give her what she "needed"? Oh, Seppy dear, why didn't I believe . . . (she thought)?

She looked at Sledge. "I'm not impressed," she said, talking fast, so she'd be doing something (other than, say, jumping up and screaming). "*I* think the Bible says you shouldn't judge, or you'll be judged yourself. And it seems to me that Jesus said He *loved* all children, specially. An' didn't He *forgive* the prostitutes and tax collectors, even, an' save the woman they were going to stone to death? Mercy and forgiveness and love is what He talked about that *I* remember. Not beating people up." She put the rod down on the floor beside her. Once again, she'd tried to sound offhand, impersonal, and she was not about to look at Omar.

Sledge smiled. "You seem to know some scripture, Miss Maria. Jesus *had* a wimp side to him; we're not too big on that. But surely you'll have heard that 'He who spares the rod, hates his child. . . .' *That's* from the Book of Proverbs. *We* don't hate our children, here" — that reasonable hand came out again — "and so we prove it to them in the best and clearest way imaginable. 'Woe unto them that call evil good and good evil.' That's from our ancestor Isaiah; I urge you to remember it. And also, 'Whip the devil out of children' — *I* said that. Although the child may feel a sting or two, it's old Beelzebub who takes the beating."

He looked away again, back to that farthest corner of the room, his source, apparently, the place he got the word from. *Other* people were possessed by demons (he believed), but Sledge, he was inhabited by God (and you could ask him).

"Now getting back to this small town of yours," he said. "I have some other questions and advice for you — we can come back to the rod as need be. I understand that you've been holding classes in whatever junk it is the sons of Israel believe, and also in that dopey-popey crap the Catholics think. Well, listen up: 'The dwelling of the righteous man is stripped of all abominations.' That's another one of mine." He smiled. "Isn't it a dandy? What's good

166

about it is, it means, like, anything you want it to. It *could* refer to different types of clothing, or ideas, or decorations, music — hey, you name it. In this case . . . well, we're talking heresy. The stuff they used to burn 'em at the stake for, like a taste of hell ahead of time, I guess." There was a sound from over on his other side. "You want to add a word here, Brother Omar?"

"In fairness," said the sheriff, "I should testify about those classes. What I said to you before *was* true — someone at the town suggested that they learn some things about the Jewish and the Catholic religions. But what I found out since is that it was just so folks could get right clear on what the *danger* was. Like — know your enemy? To beat the devil, you must understand his ways?"

Sledge nodded; *he'd* said that, he was pretty sure. One of his *beat*-attitudes, it sounded like.

"Well," Omar continued, "what happened was that Miss Maria, here, and all the rest of them, decided that they knew enough already. All they had to know. If you can *smell* cow-flop, and then you *see* cow-flop, you don't — now, truly — have to *taste* the stuff."

Sledge smiled. Maria couldn't quite believe how "country" Omar was, out there — how skillfully the master of psychology had made himself fit in. *She* made herself keep still, and didn't look at him, some more.

Sledge did, though. He had a further question. "But you *did* say, didn't you, that they had niggers living there, right in amongst the rest of them?"

"Well, yes," the sheriff said. "But that's because there isn't any other place for them *to* live, if you take my meaning. It isn't that they're all the same, I don't believe. Why, four–five days ago, when I was there, one of 'em was cleaning tables and the other two was scrubbing pots and pans. It seems like that they're kept in place."

Maria sat there looking at her hands. This was sort of like an encore; Omar at the microphone, herself — or, anyway, Mariasburg — the beneficiary. The first time, at the Forum, most of what he'd said had been, generally, true. At least the main points, or the points at issue, had been; Mariasburg was not a druggie town. What he'd said just now was utter bullshit, though. The black kids at the town were just the same as everybody else. Naturally. Of course. And that trash he'd talked about religion at the town — what he'd said, or anyway implied, about *her* knowing all she had to know to hate all Jews and Catholics — that was not just lying, that was slander. Sis would never have a bigot for a daughter.

But how about a coward? (Maria asked herself). She, who'd never been afraid to be herself and say what she believed, was now afraid. And Omar knew it. He had put the fear in her, by using this man Sledge, this lunatic. If she chose to contradict him now — on any point — the town would be endangered. And, no doubt, her . . . self, as well. Maria thought she might get sick or faint, if she stayed sitting there.

"Excuse me." She directed this at Sledge, struggling to keep the same unruffled voice, Miss Total Cool. "I need to use the bathroom." Maybe if she got a drink of water, she'd feel better. She even wished, confusedly, that she could get her period;

that confounded lots of men, she thought, maybe men like these. Of course she knew that wasn't going to happen.

Sledge nodded. "The nearest one is right back off the kitchen," he replied. "You just help yourself."

She went back down the hall into the kitchen. The girl Naomi was still there, alone, standing by the sink now, washing canning jars. She looked up when she heard Maria's footsteps, and when she saw just who it was — or wasn't — her eyes (just for a moment) lightened. Or so Maria thought. But then Naomi dropped them quickly, and went on with her work.

Maria said again, "I need to use the bathroom," and then she added "Hi," and hurried into it and closed the door. She took a drink of water, several deep breaths. There was a mirror there; she looked like hell. The way intimidated people always look, in addition to their *looks*, like slightly gray and grungy. The way that Sledge's wives and daughters looked.

That made her mad. Looking that way, being seen that way. No wonder that Naomi looked away. She's seen the change in her, what those two guys had done to her, Maria.

She came out of the bathroom, walked directly to the sink, and touched the girl, just lightly, on the inside of her elbow.

"I'm going to find a way to get you out of here," she whispered. "I've heard what sort of things they've done to you, and somehow I am going to get you out. And you can live with me — as long as that seems good to you. Just hang on and tell yourself it's going to happen."

Naomi stood there frozen, letting the water run, not washing jars. Maria wondered if she'd just made the biggest miscalculation of her entire life; these people here were this girl's *family*. "God is *love*," she said, "not beatings. Just nod if you would like to get away from here. I promise you I'll help you if you want me to."

Nothing happened for another moment. Maria tried to think what she would do if (just for instance) this Naomi, here, were suddenly to start to scream for Daddy — tellin' him what this ol' Satan pedermaster just now said.

And then Naomi nodded. Not once and barely, but *two* times, and forcefully, good hard up-and-downs.

Maria squeezed her arm this time. "It may take weeks, but it'll happen. It's a promise." And frightened she'd been gone too long already, she hurried back to where the two men waited.

They were talking in low voices when she came back in the room, Omar leaning forward, maybe pushing something hard at Sledge's ear; his County Sheriff's star gleamed brightly on his breast.

Maria sat back down and crossed her legs, leaned back, noticing the rod beside her chair had disappeared.

She stayed there another hour, mostly listening to Sledge as he described the final battle. It was as if he'd heard enough about the town, or gotten bored with it. That battle was another story, though. It looked as if he'd never weary of that subject.

It would include, so he predicted (rather merrily, she thought) both nuclear and conventional forces, and would end with the total destruction of the earth ("all life, including roaches"), with the planet ending up as only so much cosmic dust. Sometime before the final, biggest-ever Bang, he and his cohorts would be plucked from off their tractor seats, of course, and taken straight to heaven and the rapture they had coming to them. He said that right at the moment, he didn't know for sure if he'd be seeing her and all her friends in Paradise. He said he maybe thought that they — like certain of his children (names unspecified) — were "tweenies," still; beings who were unresolved and incomplete, "Who hadn't got their tickets, yet, one way or the other."

What he said he *had* decided was to leave her (and the other people in her town) "under Brother Omar's watchful eye, some more." Brother Omar would continue to report to him, tell him how the town was shaping up. And he, before the Day, would know what needed to be done, or not.

" 'Serve the Lord with fear, rejoice with trembling,' " he said to her, instead of "See ya," or "So long." She hadn't seen *him* tremble much, so far.

A minute later, they were in the squad car, heading out of there.

20

Driven

They rode away from the big stone house in silence. Maria rolled her window down and turned her head away from Omar slightly, looking out. Sitting in the draft that blustered through that way-wide-open window made her feel less joined to him, more separate, in a different world, almost. She put her elbow on the sill. At least the summer air, coming off the growing fields and pasture all around the house, smelled good. The car went steadily downhill, not fast but steadily. *Just keep on going, please don't stop*, she told the car.

Maria pressed down with her elbow on the windowsill. She flapped it up and down, flirting with the danger of a wallop on the funny bone, just as a distraction. She tried to figure out how she would make it through that window, if she had to. Probably a headfirst dive was best, followed by a sort of breaststroke through the thing, then try to duck her head, like in a somersault, and roll. But opening the door would probably be faster yet, assuming that she could. Possibly, he had the means to lock it from his side. She wondered if perhaps there was a motor on her window, too. That'd be just great:

to dive and have the window, rising, trap her half-way in and halfway out. Omar'd have a ball with his half, there inside the car; what a chance to give it what it "needed," with her pants around her ankles, with his doubled leather belt.

The boy, that Japhet, must have seen them coming. He had the steel gate open by the time they got to it, so Omar didn't have to blow his horn, or even slow the car before he passed on through. He tossed the boy a little wave, a lefty half salute, as he went by. Japhet never caught it, though, Maria noticed. He was staring at his boot toes all the time.

Next, she thought of trying to start a conversation, just to make the time go by, but very soon she canceled that idea. Sis had brought her up to think about another person's feelings, but otherwise to speak her mind. ("This is America," Sis said, "and children are Americans the same as grown-ups are. Except when their dear mothers want to use the telephone, at which point they are cheese mold.") But this was not a time for frankness, or revelations — and Omar's feelings were exactly what she didn't want to think about, just then.

They turned off the Defenders' private road and started toward Mariasburg. Maria took a nice deep breath and let it out again. Her body felt all stiff and strange to her, and she still had nothing that seemed right to say. It was just a matter of miles, she told herself. In so many miles and after such-and-such a number of minutes, this'd all be over. Assuming that Omar didn't get a flat or ("Gee. . . .") run out of gas, that is.

"You really showed me something in the pluck department, there, the way you talked to Sledge," said Omar. He said that in a chatty and enthusiastic tone of voice. It sounded like the guy was picking up a thread of conversation, rather than presenting new material.

"I really did admire you for that," he said. "You know, for weeks he'd talked about how he was gonna whip you good, himself, with me to hold you down and help. He said that even if you didn't need the cure, he'd lay some good prevention on you. And once he saw you, he had other reasons, too, I'm sure." Omar shook his head. "I was going to let him go ahead and do it." He chuckled, maybe at that (former) foolishness of his. "For reasons of my own, I guess. I knew it wouldn't kill you. But when you stood up to him like that, it really got to me how much I liked you. I didn't want just anyone, like Sledge, to see . . . *you* know, my girlfriend. So I told him that he couldn't do it. Told him he'd be putting me, as County Sheriff, in an untenable position. You weren't any kid of his, nor had you broken any laws. Not man's *nor* God's, as far as we knew. So I said I couldn't let him do it after all."

"Well," Maria said. "I guess I ought to thank you, then."

She got the words out quickly, just to break her silence, show them both she hadn't lost her voice or gone into a silent sulk. She sounded sort of hoarse, to her own ears, a little rusty. She barely could believe her ears. His *girlfriend*? Could he possible believe. . . ?

That didn't matter. All that mattered was for her to find a way of acting that would get her out of there and safely home. *Act*, she told herself, and partway turned toward him, and smiled a partway smile. She meant the smile to be ironic, slightly put-upon, expressing just a tinge of boredom. A *complicated* smile, friendly but untouchable — and fearless. Aloof, a little regal, yet not snooty or annoying. *There!* — she thought she had it. So, move over, Meryl-baby.

"No 'ought to's'," Omar said. "There aren't any 'ought to's' in a real relationship. People do things for each other, 'cause they want to. And that's the way it should be with the two of us."

"Of course," Maria murmured, softly — *distantly*, she hoped. *Want not, want not, want not*, she told herself — another Roches song.

Omar sucked a deep breath of his own and let it out in one quick bark of laughter.

"I guess I might as well admit it," he went on. "At first, when I came up to the town, I *was* just trying to score. On you and Mimi, both. Hell, you can take that as a compliment, looked at in a certain light. Down in Hoops, the usual's the other way around. Girls come in the County Courthouse, there, and want to do it in the solitary cells with me. I kid you not — can you imagine? One thin blanket on a ce-ment floor? Girls all call me 'Sheriff No' behind my back, down there.

"But anyway," he said. "I've gone way past those early feelings, now. I really like you . . . Mya. That's what Seppy calls you sometimes, doesn't he? That's cute." He grabbed another breath. "I think I like you more than any gal I've ever met. It's almost kind of scary, what I'm feeling. You've just got so much *style*, you know? Such a way of handling yourself. Like with that father at the Forum, there, and now — just now — with Sledge. I think we're lots the same, you know? We both are take-charge people, leaders, people who perform well under pressure."

He'd laid his hat down on the seat between them, but now he put it on again, and set it at an angle.

"I was just like that at your age, too. I'm only thirty now, if you were wondering. Still feel like a kid, in lots of ways that count." He winked and smiled — and waited.

"Yes, I've noticed that," Maria said. She tried to keep her voice in neutral. To give him nothing he could cuddle up to or get angry at.

"In terms of how I see the world and how I run my life," said Omar, "and the things I like to do for fun, I'm more like eighteen, still. You probably have noticed that, as well. The way I fit in at the town with all the boys. I don't believe they see me as an older guy at all. Do you?"

"I wouldn't really know," Maria said. "I haven't heard that talked about a lot." That sounded . . . fair, she told herself. Pleasant, yes, but still across the hall from "chummy." She hoped he'd cool it with the questions.

"Well, how about yourself?" the sheriff asked (of course). "You see I'm not that bad, now, don't you? That I'm just mostly trying to help you and the town?"

Good Lord, she thought, three zingers. She wished that she could laugh hysterically. She imagined what her script would look like: MARIA (Meryl Streep) *laughs hysterically. . . . Not that bad?* A looney-tune who got his jollies whipping teenaged kids? A maniac who'd just now told her he was going to hold her down so Sledge could beat on *her*? An ego-case who probably believed that she was *also* wishing they could check into a solitary cell right now, Sheriff and Mrs. 34891, no luggage.

But such a script was not available, and so she pursed her lips and tried to change the subject.

"Well, I *guess*," she finally said. "Though some of what you said back there" — she jerked a thumb toward where they'd been — "sounded pretty KKK-ish. Do you believe that kind of junk, or were you playing games with Sledge, or what?"

Omar leaned back hard against the seat, pushed with both his hands against the steering wheel, and smiled.

"I believe a little bit of everything," he said. "The same as almost everybody else does. The same as even you do, too, if you're as normal as I think you are. Everybody has some attitudes, some thoughts and fantasies that aren't all that . . . *proper*, you could say. (This isn't guesswork; what I'm talking here is research, scientific fact.) But mostly folks don't put them into words, out loud. Mostly, I don't either. Because of practical considerations; there isn't any point in roiling up the waters. I *know* the voters in my county, there, are every bit as bigoted, and this-and-that, as I am. And that almost all of them have got a mental list of folks they'd like to see stone dead, or bare-ass naked on a beach towel.

"That's our little secret," Omar said, and winked again. "That I know lots of stuff that's going through their minds — that I have studied up on it. They know I know, all right. So all I have to do is smile at them a certain way and they will pull my lever for me — on election day, of course." He turned his head to glance at her.

"I don't care for Jews and niggers, no," he said. "And as far as I'm concerned the Catholics are a moron bunch of dressed-up, superstitious hypocrites. But hell, I'm not that keen about, oh, middle westerners or Baptists, any bunch of people, anywhere. Human nature is the same, no matter what the label on 'em reads. We all have Jack the Ripper in us, *and* whatever saint you want to name. Hitler, he was crazy 'cause he let his Jack-the-Ripper side go wild; he overdid it, you could say. But here's what folks don't like to face: so were so-called saints like Gandhi crazy. They were equally unbalanced, but the other way. You see that — what I'm getting at?" Omar waited while it all sank in.

"There you go," he said, when he was sure it had.

There you go. Maria said that over to herself, silently, inside her head. *There you go.* She'd just had Omar's explanation of himself, of everyone. He wasn't any lech or bigot, only human. Anything he said or did was simply an expression of this normal human self of his. Anything he chose to do was *justified* by that. He couldn't help it, man; humanity had made him do it, he was simply Everyman, in history. She had to see he wasn't all that bad. Maybe, just at times, a little *naughty*, but that's all — same as she might be. But that was unavoidable. *There you go*, he'd said.

"I know you're just like me," said Omar, now, "and that's all right. It really is. It's really pretty wonderful, in fact, and I can help you *face* that fact, and others like it, too. There's nothing that you have to be ashamed about. Maybe for a little while, at first, you'll feel a little, like, embarrassed. If you do, that's normal, psychologically. It comes from having been brought up a certain way, from being told you have to push the one side of yourself, and bite back on the other one."

Maria didn't know if it was his fantastic timing or just luck, but at the moment Omar finished saying that, he swung the squad car off the highway onto still another unmarked road.

"Where are we going?" (naturally) she asked. (*Not* "Oh, is this a shortcut?") Her throat felt extra, extra dry.

"To check out a fantastic view," he said. "And let you do us both a favor."

The road wound through some scrubby growth, then widened, unexpectedly, and stopped. Omar wasn't kidding, not about the scenery, at least. Spread before them was a postcard manufacturer's delight, an absolutely top-ten vista, miles and miles of light and shadow, looking down the wild and narrow San Wakhaki valley.

"I agree," said Omar, "that it's good for us to keep our books in balance, our accounts. You said it first, yourself — remember? — that you ought to thank me for the things I've done for you today." He held his left hand up so as to count them on those fingers.

"Taking you to Sledge's so's he wouldn't come to your Mariasburg and maybe get some weird ideas. Telling him a few white lies about exactly what goes on back there. And, thirdly, keeping his mean switches and his eyeballs off your rump. Plus, finally, on top of all of that, I've . . . well, confided in you, absolutely. Cut the crap — you know? — and let you see exactly who I am, no masks on and no games. And now I'm telling you I *love* you, Mya.

179

So, totally without an 'ought to' in the world, you know that it's all right for you to love me back, beginning now."

With which he smiled and hitched his body half around, so he was almost facing her. The hand that he'd been counting with had dropped down on the buckle of his belt.

Maria didn't see the sense of waiting for the floor show, the rest of the "fantastic view." She snatched the twelve-gauge off the dashboard rack, aimed it at the windshield right between the two of them, and pulled the trigger.

The noise was unbelievable. Maria'd never known sound as that kind of force before, never had been *struck* by sound, engulfed, left dizzy and in major pain by it. The other physical effects were also unexpectedly spectacular: the windshield went from clear to crazy, still in place but crisscrossed by ten thousand lines that made it look like diamonds pressed together, with just the one no-more-than-grapefruit-sized round hole in it, right there in its middle.

She couldn't think or hear; the pain was still too strong and new, unprecedented. She felt like she'd been skewered, ear to ear. But still she kept on acting, doing what came naturally, it seemed. She pulled the slide below the barrel of the shotgun back. The empty shell ejected. She pumped the slide back forward, got another round in place. (Who says you can't learn useful stuff on nighttime network television?) The gun was pointed right at Omar's chest, now. She reached and took the pistol from his holster, tossed it out her window.

"If you pull that zipper far enough to let an *earth-*

worm out, I'm going to shoot you where your lunch would be," Maria said, "if Sledge was any kind of host." She couldn't really hear her voice, except all muffled in her head.

The sheriff looked to be in shock, completely petrified. Instinctively, he'd thrown his body back (reacting to the blast), and so his head was stretched away from her as far as it would go. His chin had almost disappeared into his neck; his eyes were wide and focused on the barrel of the gun. Instead of tan, his skin looked greenish-yellow.

"Be careful with that thing," he finally croaked. He sounded, to Maria, like a person being strangled in a closet, far away. "I wasn't going to . . . anything. Can't you take a little joke for Christ's sweet sa — ?"

"Shut up," Maria said. "Just start the car. Then stick your head outside your window, there. That's how you're going to drive. If you stop the car, or go too fast, or try to pull your head inside, I'm going to blow you right in half, you understand?" She and Meryl finally had their laugh, but passed on the "hysterical." "I'm sure a jury would applaud me for a job well done. So drive."

He started up the car and did as he was told. He got them out of there and back onto the road they'd come by, heading for Mariasburg. When they were a short way from the town — a quarter mile or less below it, but around a curve — she jabbed him with the gun and made him stop the car.

"Get out," she said. "Real slowly." He opened up his door and clambered out, more awkward than she'd ever seen him. She followed, turning off the key and taking it, as she went by. She made him walk into the woods and sit down on a boulder; she stayed standing, maybe fifteen feet away.

"Okay," said Omar. "Game and set and match." He said that sharp and stuttery; he tried to smile. "You win. I'm through. That's it. I'll never come up here again without an invitation, that's a promise. You can keep the gun and shoot me if I do. Frankly, I've completely lost the thing I had for you, the love I thought that I was feeling. I only hope you haven't broken my damn eardrums."

Maria thought *he* thought that she was (maybe) going to shoot him — hence this sweet surrender, this complete fulfillment of her wildest, dearest dreams. All that remained was one quite simple question: could she trust him (in the slightest)?

Well, possibly she could — she and Meryl, that'd be. She'd walk back into town, disheveling along the way, and tell the kids a story of attempted rape (not really all that big a lie). Combine what she would say with her appearance and the note he'd posted on the church a few weeks back (she'd kept the thing as a memento) and Mimimi's description of their walk around the grounds (and all that Omar'd said and done, including grabbies at the end), and there would be a case against the guy, for sure. He'd come to trial, there'd be a scandal; even if a jury found him innocent (Oh, no — not Sheriff No!), he'd surely lose his reputation and his job.

She told him all of this. That he had better do *exactly* as he'd just now said he would. She laid out the "or else" in Technicolored detail. He said he understood and that she'd never have to use that story ("frame him," as he chose to put it). A practicing psychologist, he said, knew when to cut off

182

an . . . experiment. He understood, and lived within, the limits of a situation.

She said that she'd be leaving, then. She threw the car keys off into the woods and vanished in the opposite direction. Even if he had a rifle in the trunk, he never would have time to use it — not before she'd got to town and told the kids her story. Once she'd done that, he wouldn't dare to shoot her.

Incredibly, she thought, this all could turn out for the best. Mariasburg would have its sheriff (for protection) but. . . . She and Mimimi would laugh about that later. You always laugh about these kinds of situations later, so the story goes.

21

An Honest Bang

"Hey, Georgie. Howza boy?"

The Hupee County Clerk removed the telephone that he'd been holding to his ear and looked at it disgustedly. He crinkled up his nose and sniffed, as if (perhaps) a mouse had died in the receiver.

Of course he'd recognized the voice. Even if he hadn't, no one else had ever called him "Georgie," other than his mother. His mother and this whippersnapper, here. And no one else tossed out a "Howza boy?" to him, a man of eighty-two, a living legend, clerk for fifty-seven years and never set a foot outside the county, all that time. He wondered where the governor had found the whippersnapper, and what possessed him to appoint him as his personal executive assistant. Of course there were a lot of things that one-time heavyweight contender J. P. "Punch" Palattice did as governor that made no sense in Hupee County.

"I'm taking nourishment." He said that drily to the telephone, holding it in proper place again. "I'm at my desk by seven every morning, and I still do all the ledger work in pen and ink, by hand. So chances are I'm still among the living."

The telephone receiver cackled in his ear.

"Same old Georgie," said the 'snapper. "Still got your sensa humor. And that same old rolltop desk, I bet. But anyway — hey, look. Punch axed me if I'd buzz you on this deal. I'm looking at a copy of a letter from a real dear friend of his. 'RELCO, Inc.,' the letterhead? Electrical Contractors? Wanting us to check on some small town up there? Name of Jacks-'r-better, right?"

"Yes?" the County Clerk said, cautiously. His memory was perfect, always had been; that letter was a piece of typical presumptuousness from some conceited, self-important meddler who'd come up there from Cinverguenza way to tell the folks in Hupee County how to run their business. The clerk had written back a note which said the questions raised would be both carefully and prayerfully considered — with any necessary steps to follow. Then he'd filed the letter and a carbon of his note inside a folder labeled "Processed Garbage." Period; case closed.

"Well, Punch just wanted you to know he'll run the ball himself on that one," said the whipper-snapper, now. "You don't have to bother with the thing a-tall. We're going to send a few folks up to check the situation out, next week: people from Child Welfare, Education, Safety, Sanitation, and the State Police and so on. Save you County boys some time and trouble, I imagine. They'll give us a complete report, chop-chop, and naturally you'll have one for your files. Plus copies of whatever actions end up being taken as a consequence. It ought to be a real attractive item. We're thinking color photographs, as well as illustrations, graphs, and so on, with the scenery up there. Punch is darn excited by the project, I can tell you."

"And if it happens he goes on into that senate race. . . ," the Hupee County Clerk began.

"Hey, Georgie, cut that out, you scamp," the personal executive assistant said, around another set of giggles. "Punch gives an honest bang for every buck, that's true. But as far as 1990 is concerned. . . . Well, hey, we'd like to have your input on that possibility, seeing as you brought it up. Maybe we can do a lunch around that theme sometime, okay? Awright? You bet. We love you, babe." And he hung up.

The Hupee County Clerk did likewise, with a sneer. He didn't doubt that Punch was going to run for senator. This "raid" on Jacks-'r-better might be good for some publicity, he reckoned. Give some kids the business; put them in their place. Everybody liked to see that happen. Meanwhile, he'd forget about the matter, put it from his mind, again. Waste of time and money, far as he believed. The State could do whatever it damn pleased; no need to take up county workers' time with nonsense of that nature, picking on a bunch of kids. Hell, he had been a kid himself, as he remembered — and quite a feisty little whippersnapper, too.

22

Directions

Sis recognized the girl, although she'd only seen her once before. Maria'd talked about her, later, quite a bit. Funny name she had, like Tootie or some such.

"Sure," Sis said, "come in. Of course I do. Except I didn't see you at the Open House. Where were you hiding, all that time? Or didn't you go up there, after all?"

"No," said Sookie, "I went up, all right. But then I *messed* up, too. Just like a crazy idiot. I really blew it, I'm not kidding. I guess you haven't heard."

Sis shook her head and closed the door behind the girl, who didn't look messed up at all. Especially compared to last time. She had a nice white camp shirt on, a pair of yellow shorts; her hair was clean and shiny and her eyes were bright. Sis's feelings put their hand up to be heard: this girl was A-OK.

"Maria kicked me out," the girl continued. Sis looked borderline incredulous. "I guess I'd planned on leaving anyway, but maybe coming back; *she* told me I was through for good. She was completely justified. I didn't deserve that place, is what the truth is."

187

"Look, I'll make some tea," Sis said. Then, slyly, "Or would you rather have a beer?"

"No, tea'd be just great. You're sure you've got the time?" said Sookie. She was feeling pretty nervous, now that she was there. "I just had to ask you this one thing. Well, maybe two things, actually — depending."

They went into the kitchen. Sis got out mugs and spoons and started water boiling, what Maria would have called her "mother's-in-the-kitchen" bit.

"Well, whatever you've been doing, it agrees with you," she said to Sookie. "You look wonderful."

"Compared to when you saw me last — right?" Sookie dropped her eyes and laughed a little, just a social sound. "I started feeling better at Mariasburg. That place was really great for me. I exercised and ate three meals a day and hung out with some real nice kids, and even did some stuff for other people. But then. . . ." She shook her head and smiled, and sighed. "But then I started going with this boy up there — a real cute boy, I thought — and he had drugs and pretty soon we . . . *you* know. And Maria, she found out somehow, and hit the roof." She looked at Sis and did a little number with her eyes.

"Well. It turned out the boy — his name was Connie — he couldn't stand it up there, anyway. So that was fine with him, to leave right after that. I thought he liked me more than he turned out to, though. Soon as we got back, he started running with his other friends, like, different girls from his old neighborhood, and all. And more or less ignoring me. Finally, just last week, he took off for Australia."

"No kidding. Wow," said Sis. "Australia." She'd heard that song before, but not *Australia*. She took the kettle off the stove and poured. "Funny thing about a summer romance — a lot of times it don't survive the bus ride, coming home. A customer was telling me about these people down in South America (I think it was) who live way high up in the mountains. He said if they come down to normal altitude, they just get sick and die. Like summer love, right? It seems to work best in the mountains. Or at the seashore, come to think of it." She sighed. "Go figure," she suggested, and she shrugged and lighted up a Salem, which she laid down in an ashtray featuring our Lady Liberty, standing on the edge.

"But anyway," said Sookie. "Long before he left, I wasn't seeing him. I didn't even want to. I started taking care of me, instead — like I'd been doing at Mariasburg. Eating right and doing an aerobics class. I was staying with my aunt, who is a *real* nice lady, and I even got a job." She stirred some honey in her tea. "It's cocktail waitressing. Not like the real thing, what you do, from what Maria said. At all. It's down at ——." She named the place; Sis nodded. The tips were great down there; the hours and conditions just about unbearable. The girls who waitressed there were not professionals. Not at waitressing, they weren't.

"I'm amazed you look so great," Sis said. Then smiled. "I just mean the hours and all." She didn't want the girl to think that *she* thought . . . *you* know.

"I don't think I can stand it a whole lot longer," Sookie said. "But I had to make some money. And

I wanted . . . well, to sort of give myself a test. Prove I wasn't just a total boob — some kind of a compulsive. I didn't think I was an addict, *yet*; this seemed like one way to find out." She took a real deep breath and smiled. "Well, now I've proved that to myself, and so I want to go and tell Maria. Thank her. Tell her that I'm sorry, too. That's if you think there's any point."

Sookie dropped her eyes and shook her head again.

"The thing is this," she said. "We didn't part on real good terms. I was pretty mean . . . some things I said. So what I wondered is: d'you think it'd be best if I just bagged it? Rather than show up, out of the blue, and try to talk to her, explain? Tell her what all's happened? I wouldn't blame her if she didn't want to talk to me, just started screaming, or whatever."

"Hell," said Sis, "that's not Maria. She isn't perfect; no one is." She smiled. "But in spite of all the ways I tried to ruin her, she's still got *some* good qualities, I must admit. For instance, she's a lover *and* an optimist; she just believes in happy endings. She really cared about you . . . *Sookie*, isn't it? I've never been real good at names. And so she'll never stop, not till she gets her happy ending. That's just the way she is. I'd bet a week of tips on it."

Sookie nodded, smiled; she looked as if she'd like to clap her hands. She then asked Sis about directions, getting there; her aunt would lend a car. Sis did her best. She always *thought* she knew the way to places, although from time to time, at work, she'd get all turned around and end up in the alley with a tray of prime rib specials.

190

23

Plans A and B

It's hard to do an imaginative disheveling job rushing through some woods, without a mirror. Maria stuck to the basics: a smear of dirt across one cheekbone, wild unbraided hair, ripsville on the big plaid buttoned shirt. Good enough, she thought. She was talking "close call" here, not "felony statistic." She came up through the woods on the river side of town, and there were Jake and Babe behind the Armes, splitting wood for barbecues. As she had planned, Omar wasn't in the scene at all; he was still engrossed in her new version of that grand old household game called Find-the-Car-Keys.

She told them what had happened, talking fast, and then, accompanied by them and clouds of indignation, she went inside the Armes and laid her story on The Guise, who even stopped their practicing to listen. Then, shaking off expressions of solicitous concern and offers of a sandwich, coffee, company, she went up to her room and laid down on the bed. Not so much to nap or have the vapors as to just space out a little.

Of course she didn't get much past the letter "s" before a knock came on her door, followed very fast by Mimimi and Seppy. Anxious and enraged, respectively.

Maria had to smile at their expressions, although Seppy's worried her a bit.

"Not to worry, virtue fans," she said. "The bride can still wear *off*-white, anyway; no brand-new notches on the sheriff's .44. In fact and *au contraire*, the poor man's had a loss of interest, I believe it's fair to say. And possibly of hearing, too. But for a moment there, ol' Nancy Drew was lookin' pretty — "

"Start at the beginning," Seppy said. But grimly.

"Omitting no detail, however lewd, lascivious, or unbelievable to one of my *extremely* tender age and innocence," said Mimimi.

"Actually it wasn't in the least bit funny," said Maria. "Unless you weren't there, of course. Before we even got to Sledge's place. . . ." With which she told them everything, the whole, entire, sweaty-sided truth. When she was finished, there were looks of pure amazement and disgust.

"The man is *such* a scum-bag," Mimimi opined. "Excuse my unoriginality, but at the moment all the new ideas I have involve creative methods for inflicting pain on males with tendencies like Omar's. Or make that Omar in particular — himself. Here's one I like: you take a monkey wrench. . . ."

Maria smiled, but also waved a hand.

"He's crazy," she insisted. "I'm sure he's even one specific type of crazy. I wish I knew the name for it. I'll have to look it up sometime. But meanwhile I just want to lie here for a day and take deep breaths and pinch myself — not hard. And tell you guys how glad I am to be here. And tell the Sepperino he was right, and I was wrong to go at all."

"Likewise and emphatically," said Mimimi. "By which I mean. . . ."

"I know," Maria said.

"I know," said Seppy, also, listening to stuff inside his head as well as them. He was nodding, more relieved than angry now, she thought. She hoped. "And while you still remember what it felt like, we'd better talk it over here, tonight." She didn't think he looked exactly *cozy*, still.

". . . I think we got to have Plan B in place, as well," said Parmenter. "Who's to say old Omar won't just turn around and tell this Sledge and them to boogie up this way and run some tests on us; see if wooden houses burn, like that? In spite of everything that everybody's said, I think that's real damn close to *probable*, you want to know the truth."

It was after dinner, in the dining room. Discussion had been going on for just about an hour. Like Maria, lots of them believed that Omar — guys like Omar — never risk their images (or necks) if they don't have to.

"Especially," said Etta, "when someone's made the point as *graphically* as Mya did that she is no way gonna fall for his fandango."

But still, they had to think of The Defenders, too — consider what they might decide to do, or be talked into doing. To Maria, who had seen them, they were bad enough; imagined, they were even worse, some ways, though certain voices argued for . . . perspective.

"The trouble is," said Roger, slicing at the air with side-hand chops, the way that Richard Nixon used to do, "the trouble is those damn fanatics don't behave, or operate, like ordinary people, real Amur-ricans. You never see fanatics on a *game show*, right? You'd think they'd be on lots of them, like *Family Feud*, for instance. But no, they're *never* on that show, or any other one, and you know why? The producers, they won't have them, is the story. Won't touch them with a ten-foot pole. They know fanatics aren't any *fun*. There's nothing anyone can do to them to make them, like, jump up and down and holler out 'Good answer,' or get all wiggy like a normal person. Cars and money don't mean any-thing to them. It's just unnatural, is what I say."

He held himself by both his upper arms, and shivered.

"Brrr," he said. "Gives me the chills to think they might come here someday. We wouldn't have a thing to talk about, one thing in common. I *hate* those awkward silences, no kidding."

"I still think we should stay," said Sophie, pulling one peroxide curl. "If I was a Defender and believed that Armageddon might be coming soon, or any time at all, I'd play it by the book. Don't they have to wait for signs, or something? And besides, this Sledge as good as told Maria he was going to give us time to, like, develop."

"Yeah, but are you saying that because you really believe they won't come over here?" asked Boid. "Or is it that" — his voice got deep and sinister — "you can't face being home again?"

"Well," said Sophie, "I admit I love it here. Who doesn't? But, jokes aside, I'm also looking forward to the next stage of my life, to playing dates and being famous — right? — maybe getting a part-time job and having an apartment. (Don't laugh at me, Boid; I'm serious.) I don't know. I just don't want to be, like, driven out of here."

"I could stay up here forever," said Willa, dreamily. "I know I'm not going to and that I shouldn't even *want* to, in a way. But this place seems like where my life began. Before . . . I don't know, maybe it was me, but everything seemed all jumbled up. It wasn't that I thought I was so stupid, or . . . not *capable*, or stuff like that. But still, I couldn't see me making it. Doing anything constructive. Or anything at all, as a matter of fact, beside hanging around with my parents, and hating *that*. Other kids all seemed so . . . *different*, I don't know. In another world from me, like one I didn't even want to be in. I'm still not in a real big rush, but now, at least. . . ." She let the sentence drift.

Other people then chimed in. Maria got the feeling some of them were almost getting off on the occasion, this chance to say some private things in public.

"I always thought school spirit was just about the ultimate in legal dope," said Roger. "It seemed to be the junk they'd feed the peasants — you know, to keep them on the nod and off the streets. They said we ought to make our school the best, but just in ways that they decided on. No one else was meant to have ideas, to be original or different. So, naturally, I had to stay completely off that stuff, to test completely clean. It's weird when I compare that to up here. We're different as can be, but we still have lots in common. (I saw that face, E-*person*.) But back there they'd talk about cooperation, sharing, tolerance, as if they owned those words. But I could see *they* weren't tolerant, and they sure as hell did not cooperate or share with *me*. Here, it's just what life is all about, those things."

"So, where does all that leave you, oh enlightened one?" asked Mimimi.

Roger laughed. "Who knows?" he said. "More out of it than ever? Moonbait? Or how about a lobbyist for little ol' Plan A, which is we stay right here and breed until we've got enough of us to make a perfect world. I know, I know." He held up a hand. "It's hard and time-consuming work, real heavy breeding is. I don't deny it. But frankly, girls, I'm in a position to make that kind of commitment, or I soon can be if anyone. . . ." He let the throwing-up sounds drown him out.

It wasn't too long after that when Parmenter brought up the need for a Plan B, as well — what they might do in case of (to prepare for) an attack.

Laying in a good supply of weapons was the first idea brought up. And taking time to learn to use them, naturally. There was a certain charm to that idea. Certain kids could see themselves, perhaps in buckskins, graceful, silent, very lean (hips and thighs included), flitting through the forest, stopping now and then to aim and fire single shots at ravening fanatic rapists. Each shot, of course, would find its mark, causing that mistaken man (there were no female rapist/targets in their minds) to (bloodlessly) collapse and tumble down a rocky hillside, starting one (small) avalanche, which (handily) would serve to bury him (so much for mess and odor). No one on their side was ever killed or wounded, and every-one proved equally adept at throwing knives and boomerangs and using pistols, rifles, slingshots, blowguns, quarterstaves, and bows and arrows.

Once reality set in, however, all the people knew they didn't want to go that route; that they preferred some other version of Plan B.

"Perhaps we might consider *flight*, instead of fight," said Seppy, "a tactical retreat maneuver, also known as bug-out."

"How about we make some *rafts*?" said Babe. "It wouldn't be real hard to do. And that way, supposin' that they blocked the road or something, we could *float* on out of here." He looked delighted with that plan. "It'd be like in the olden days — right, Jake? — the way the 'jacks'd get the logs downstream, to where they had the mills. But now we'll end up at that Lakeside Mill Marina."

A lot of people both agreed with that and said that they should also make (and hide) some caches, filled with food and camp supplies, in case they couldn't make it to the stream and had to just disperse into the woods real fast, and scatter through the wilderness.

So, two Plan B's were generally approved, and Babe and Mimimi agreed to put them into action, starting the next day. Everybody said they'd help, The Guise included; E-Man said he'd learn the song, "The Volga Boatman." Roger said he still preferred Plan A.

24

Pleasant Dreams

Sledge hadn't been exactly thrilled when brother Omar'd said he wasn't going to let him whip the girl, Maria. First of all, as patriarch and prophet, he knew that he had every right to function as a kind of moral guide, herding all God's children up to and along the road to righteousness. As such, he'd used the rod — as well as prayers and readings and instruction — in bringing up his own fourteen, and had even permitted brother Omar to help out, when he had asked to, with Naomi. In this case, he'd expected Omar to return . . . well, not the favor, the *responsibility*. And once he'd seen the girl, the expectation fast became important, a thing a fellow could look forward to. Business didn't always mix with Sledge's pleasure — not so's he'd admit it, anyway.

Also, Sledge had not, in recent years, had anyone say "no" to him. Not for very long, or strong enough to make it stick. At Sledge's house, with Sledge's family, the only person in command, the only one who had authority, was Sledge. Him and the Lord, of course, with him the active member of the firm. And maybe, sure, his wives, on little things that had

198

to do with little kids, or who cleaned out the toilets. So, though obedience to *all* authority was stressed, when Omar pulled his rank as County Sheriff (as he'd done), Sledge had only gone along with him most grudgingly. He hadn't liked that shoe on Omar's foot at all.

Even by the time he'd gone to bed that night, he'd still been irked — the more so when he thought some more about Maria, and let himself imagine how it would have gone if Omar hadn't been there, or had kept his big yap shut. It got him pretty well excited, imagining all that. He tossed and turned a lot before he got to sleep.

Later on that night, he had a dream. In it, he was walking down the one main street in Jacks-'r-better, now Mariasburg. But it was hardly anything at all like what the sheriff had described. Hooeee! He'd never in his life seen *any* town — and he had seen some wild ones in his youth — as rotten and corrupt, as downright *evil*, as Mariasburg.

From every window blared satanic music (foul and eerie with a wham-bam beat), blended with a bunch of squeals, and giggles of delight. Couples danced along the sidewalk, drinking out of open jugs and bottles; pigs and serpents rolled and writhed with them in gutters. Boys and girls of every different race that you could think of were paired up with one another and *each* other, fondling and kissing, messing with each other's clothes. There were the smells of perfume and of incense in the air, along with those of luscious, fresh-baked cakes and pies, and smoke from different kinds of funny cigarettes.

Suddenly, the girl Maria just appeared in front of him, standing in the middle of the street. She smiled at him, and then she turned around and stuck her tongue out, chin up on her shoulder, looking back toward him. She didn't have no pants on, neither. He recognized his opportunity — his target and his duty — and reached out for her.

Even as he did so, chains of lightning forked from out the darkened sky, followed milliseconds later by a thunderous explosion. Before his eyes, one bolt of lightning bounced from off the steeple of the church and onto the connected wooden buildings partway down the street. A shingled roof burst into flame, and pretty soon the flames were spreading, house to house and then, in one huge licking leap, across the street. The revelers, many now buck-naked (Sledge observed) were fleeing, screaming, down that self-same street, dodging, getting struck by, burning timbers, other lightning bolts, and probably a hunk or two of brimstone. When he looked back to where she'd been, the girl, Maria, wasn't there. She'd disappeared, but in her place there was a serpent from the gutter, swallowing a pig — a pig that had an apple in its mouth.

A moment later, Sledge (now wide awake) was sitting up in bed, perspiring profusely. Outside, a mighty wind threw rain against his bedroom windows; lightning, bright as any flashbulb, showed him the familiar contents of the room; a great "ker-ACK!" of thunder, right straight overhead, brought him out of bed and to his knees.

Buried deep inside some wrinkled fold in Sledge's brain was the idea that in addition to being the strong arm of the Lord, he was also a lot like this guy Hannibal Smith, on that TV show *The A-Team*.

They both knew lots about all sorts of firearms, right up to cannons, and were partial to cigars, good-looking females, and a plan that came together; they both had leadership ability coming out their bippies. Then, too, they both were real sly foxes, the kind who didn't tip their hands ahead of time, who maybe might *appear* to do what someone else had said, but in the end did just as they had planned to, all along.

So on the next day, at the end of breakfast time, he told the family (including Josh and Enos) that he had had a vision in the night, that the Lord had chosen this device to tell him what they had to do, the older boys, the other men, and him. It was a bold and simple plan, as he explained it, combining something educational and right to do — something that had needed doing all along — with something that was damned good practice for the future. Even the smallest children understood when he explained it, he felt sure. And if the wives or older girls had any reservations, they were much too smart to make them known to him, or even blink.

25

State Inspection

Maria, former Queen of Pizza, had had a slender slice that day at lunch, for openers. But she was stuffing a small piece of whole wheat pita bread with salad that contained both onions and garbanzos when, quite by chance, she raised her eyes and saw the group of six that stood there in the doorway.

"Whoops," she said, not loud, but loud enough so Willa, Babe, and Etta all stopped working on their own nutrition long enough to look at her, and then across the room, to see what she was whoopsing at.

The six had dressed that morning as they would for any workday. That meant the state policeman wore his uniform, which showed he was a corporal, and the good-luck ankle bracelet that he'd gotten from a friend. Licensing and Sanitation both wore summer slacks with sports coats; Sanitation had a white belt and a necktie on, and Licensing was fat and did without the belt and tie; instead, he clutched a black cigar. Fire and Safety (all in one) had no jacket on, but he did sport both a western thong (that had a silver longhorn slide) around his neck and a baseball cap with *Maui* on the front of it. The longhorn's eyes were turquoise, which also was the color of the cap. The younger of the women wore a brightly flowered shirt with tight, black, tailored pants, and pumps; she was from Child Welfare. Education had a neat tan suit, with skirt, lapel watch and those big, round, lightly tinted glasses that go squiggle on the sides.

Education and the State Police both carried attaché cases. Sanitation, Licensing, and Fire and Safety all had sharp, thin leather briefcases with retractable handles. Child Welfare had a zippered nylon bag, the same color as her pants; it also had a shoulder strap.

They'd come in two cars, all the men in the policeman's cruiser with the flashers on the roof, and the two women in Child Welfare's little Mazda sports coupe. It was a long ride from the state capital, even at the speeds they'd driven; Licensing was hungry as a bear, and Education had to piss.

Sanitation peered around the dining room. He couldn't locate anyone who seemed to be in charge, who looked as if they could be in authority. He was getting ready to back out when Education stepped up to the nearest table, chose a serving spoon, and clinked the nearest glass.

The room fell silent, as she'd known it would. She collected all their eyes before she spoke, just as she'd always done the years she'd taught fifth grade.

"Good afternoon, boys and girls," she said. "I'm Mrs. Robinson from the State Department of Education. This is Miss Delfusco of the Department of Child Welfare, Mr. Waxman. . . ."

She introduced them all, pronouncing each last

name a little louder than the other words, and very clearly.

"We're here to do a study for the governor," she said, and smiled. "Of you and of this town. You may not know this, but the state maintains a file on every town within its borders, incorporated and unincorporated alike." She smiled again. "How many of you know which kind of town *this* is?"

She put her hand up high, and so did Roger, right away, and then some others. "Two, three, four, five . . . *six*. That's really very *good*," she said. Mrs. Robinson would find the bathroom in a minute, but first she had to put the room at ease, as well as make clear the mission of the team she was a part of.

Roger kept his hand way up, but also talked before she called on him.

"Excuse me, but what's in the file?" he said.

"I'm glad you asked that question," said the Education woman. "Mr. Waxman, here — "

"Basically," the fat man said, "it's basically statistics. Population, services, facilities, businesses, and schools — like that. Plus sheets of checkoffs to be sure the laws and regulations of the State and all its agencies are being carried out. And, hey. . . ." He smiled himself. "Suppose a hungry man could beg a slice of that-there pizza? We were lookin' for a place the last half hour plus, but as you know. . . ." He reached into a pocket in his pants, got out a money clip. "We'll pay you city rates, whatever you guys say is fair."

Two things happened while he spoke. When he described this "file," all the 'burgers checked each other out, but darkly, passing back and forth the "uh-oh" look. But as soon as he confessed to hunger, table-room was quickly made for six, plates and silverware provided (mugs and napkins, too), and salad bowls and serving dishes hustled over. Lisa, quietly approached, led both strange women to the nearest bathroom, and for a little while the room relaxed. A new and different challenge to Mariasburg's self-image, and its hospitality, was being neatly met.

As the visitors were feeding, the residents — most of whom had finished eating anyway — surrounded them, sitting on top of nearby tables, or even standing on the chairs for a better view. *Why had these six people come? What's the story here? Who had sent them, anyway? Why now?* Questions such as those were rattling the bars in everybody's mind. *What are they trying to do to us?*

But what was talked about, while lunch was being eaten, was the weather and the food, the mountains and the wildlife in them, how poorly marked the roads were. The state policeman said he'd get on someone down at Highways, over that one. Everybody said the food was great.

At last, when second cups of coffee had been almost drained, Fire and Safety looked around at all the faces and he said, "So tell me this. There really aren't any adults in this town at all?"

He got a lot of "no's" and some first lines of explanation, and several "*I* turned eighteen (two–three–four) months ago's."

"Let's not get technical," he said. "I'm talking people my age. Like your parents."

"No," Maria said. "There isn't anybody here like that."

The six all looked at one another, then all looked away. There was a sigh or two, a deep breath being taken. All of them stood up, like people with a job to do.

"We might as well begin," said Sanitation. "The rest of you can go about your business" — kids were not his business — "except we'll all need guides. People who can show us things and give us answers to the questions that we'll have. You must have officers, perhaps some sort of student council." His voice suggested "*someone* who's responsible." And also: "This is just ridiculous."

Maria looked at him and shook her head.

"No," she said, "we're all Young Anarchists for Freedom." But then she smiled and looked straight in his eyes, and he surprised himself by smiling back. "I'm only joking," she went on, "but anybody here can tell you anything you need to know, no problem."

"Tell you what," said Mr. Waxman, Licensing. He stood and ran his thumbs around the inside of the waistband of his slacks, and he smiled, too. That lunch had really hit the hunger-hole; what's more, he kinda *liked* these kids. "Me'n Corporal McQueen can go around together. Same with our two gracious ladies. Rebus, here" — he jerked a thumb at Sanitation — "has his own unique concerns, centered mostly on the food and septic tank departments. Gardner's got to cover the entire town for Fire and Safety, so he had better also solo — have a guide to call his very own. In other words, we'll only need to trouble four of youse. Except," he dropped his eyes and, oddly, looked embarrassed, "like, at the end, when we're all done, perhaps we'd better *all* just come together for a little while, so everyone can hear our comments and . . . suggestions."

He checked his wristwatch. "How about, say, four o'clock for that? Say, right back here again." He looked around at his five colleagues, each of whom gave little nods. They were professionals; they'd go through all the necessary motions. Before they even left for home, they'd be on double time, so that was one thing to look forward to.

What Maria did was put two guides with each of the inspectors, or each team of two. She didn't need a sock to tell which way the wind was blowing. She wanted witnesses and backups.

So, she and E-Man went with Licensing and State Police, while Mimimi and Etta took "the gals" around; Willa and Jake would stay with Sanitation, and Babe and Seppy would go on the Fire and Safety tour.

Seppy got Maria to one side before the little groups dispersed.

"This isn't an inspection, it's a fix," he said. "They're going to close us up."

"Weird," she said, and nodded. "It must mean we're successful. Or maybe this is Omar, getting back at me. Any thoughts, suggestions — maybe a last word or two?" The inspectors all were watching them, and waiting.

Seppy shrugged. E-Man, who'd come up in time to hear that last, smiled grimly.

"Yakety-yak," he told them. "Don't talk back."

26

Lost and Found

Sookie was pretty well lost when she saw the girl by the side of the road. She hadn't seen a person or a house for quite a ways, and according to Sis's estimate she should have been there long ago.

The girl looked pretty strange, and it wasn't just the long dress she had on. At first, she seemed to Sookie to be running, but then, after she had heard the car, she slowed first to a walk, and then a stroll. As Sookie got closer, she drifted off the road into a narrow patch of meadow, bent (but also turned back toward the car) as if she possibly was going to pick some flowers, but might also jump into the nearby woods and disappear.

When Sookie braked beside her, the girl stood right up straight. Sookie had to lean across the front seat to roll down the other window, and as she did, she saw the girl was holding something tight against one side, something almost hidden in the dress's folds. It looked to Sookie like a poker, the kind that people used when they had fireplaces.

"Hi," Sookie said. "I'm lost. I'm looking for a little town called Jacks-'r-better. Or Mariasburg, some people call it now. I got directions but they seem to be messed up. You ever hear of it? Mariasburg? Or Jacks-'r-better?"

The girl had just been staring at her. Almost in amazement, Sookie thought, or as if she didn't understand a word of English. Either explanation could have been the right one, it was such a big, blank, vaguely fearful sort of stare.

But then, and unexpectedly, she ran *toward* the car and (thank God, from Sookie's point of view) broke into one huge smile. A second later she had opened up the door and hurled herself inside. It *was* a poker, sure enough, but she tossed it on the floor beside her feet.

"Yes," she said. "I know the way. I have to see Maria. Do you know her?"

27

How's That?

"Well," the old man said, enjoying (as he had for fifty-seven years) the chance to tell a person something that he knew the person didn't know, " 'pears to me you'll soon have one less group of citizens in need of your protection and patrol. All I hope is that they go on paying taxes till it's sold, this time around."

"What?" said Omar, and he cocked his head a little, aiming his left ear more toward the Hupee County Clerk. He'd wandered in that office just a bit before, to check the time of the Town Council meeting. "How's that?"

"By Jiminety, I believe you're goin' *deef* on me," the County Clerk replied. "I was *saying* I suspect that bunch of kids'll soon be bidding their farewells to Jacks-'r-better. And I was wondering if they will *de*-fault on their taxes like the Sisters did, or what. Wouldn't be surprised they would, myself, as mad as I suppose they'll be."

"What makes you think the kids are going to leave?" said Omar, moving one step closer to the ancient rolltop desk, and finding that his pulse had just expressed some interest in the matter, too.

"Huh." The clerk just grunted out the word. "His *goob*natoral excellence himself, he's sicked a bunch of State Inspectors up there on them. You damn well know what that means. Them snoops could prove a convent wasn't up to code if they'd a mind to. They'd claim the sisters' beads made too much racket for the neighborhood, or the candles on the altar were a dangerous and untended hazard. Why, they've got regulations on the books that haven't made a bit of sense since back before the Civil War. They're unenforceable for one thing and illegal for another, but they're there in some department book or other, sure as hell. No, my guess is the snoops'll give the kids their thirty days to mend their violatin' ways or, failing that, be out of there. And the kids'll not have smarts or energy — or hundred-dollar bills — to fight 'em with, so they'll just fold."

Omar nodded, narrowing his eyes. *Good*, had been his first reaction, but his second had been *Maybe not so good*. Maria might believe that he had engineered this visit from the State. And that *could* set her off. Activate her whistle-blowing reflex. Make her want to cook herself some sheriff stew.

"When did you say the people from the State are making their inspection?" Omar asked. "Maybe I could put a word in for the kids. I've been up a time or two since they've been here, you know, and from what I've seen. . . ." He let his voice run down and out, completely casual.

"I didn't say," the clerk replied, moistening a thumb to turn a ledger page. "But what I *think* is anytime this week. Today's a real good possibility, but then it could have happened back on Monday. If I had to bet, I'd say today, though. Those buz-

211

zards take two days to plan a trip like this, and then they need another two to write reports about it. So *Wednesday*'d be the day to do the work, today. That way, too, they'd get their travel vouchers and their overtime recorded well before their checks are printed up. . . ." He looked up from the ledger. ". . . ON FRIDAY," he yelled out at Omar's back.

"You ill-bred, egghead, little whippersnapper," he concluded, in a *most* contented mutter.

28

Coming and Going

"I'm sure you must see now, it's nothing like a *school*," said Mimimi. The four of them, all women, she and Etta and the ones from the state Departments of Education and Child Welfare, had ended up sitting on the steps of the church, looking down Main Street and diagonally across at the hotel. They'd wandered in and out of all the buildings, and hadn't found a blackboard or a bored or battered child. They had, however, found that they could talk — communicate — about the town, and what the different kids were doing there.

"Well, yes and no," said Mrs. Robinson, of Education. "There's certainly a *structure* here, and learning going on within that structure. In terms of age, you have a population that's completely homogeneous. Everyone's expenses here — the basic ones — are being subsidized, as if you all had grants-in-aid or scholarships. And I certainly can sense a high degree of self-evaluation. To be completely honest, I'm amazed and I'm impressed." She smoothed her hair back, and she smiled at both the girls and at her colleague, Miss Delfusco. It was a different smile, in quality, than the model she had

213

shown in the dining room, when she had first arrived. This one was custom-made, from natural ingredients.

"No matter what it's called," she said, "there's plenty here that any school would love to have, I promise you."

"I'm impressed myself," said Miss Delfusco. "The more so in light of what they'd told us to expect, or what they *hinted*, anyway." She took a pack of Trident from her bag and offered it around. "My crutch," she said. "I'm two weeks into nicotine withdrawal." She fed herself two pieces, got them going.

"I was braced for *anything*." She waved a hand around. "Like, possibly, an upscale crack house — I'm not kidding — upscale in the sense of size and population, anyway. With the money for the drugs derived from, let's say, kiddie porn or prostitution. I just about fell over when I walked into your dining room and saw how everybody looked. *Then* I thought we'd lost our way and stumbled on some kinda *health spa*, I'm not kidding you." She laughed. "Any moment now, I told myself, they're gonna start to sing, like in that Coca-Cola ad. The one with all the kids up on the mountaintop?"

"So, from the point of view of what *you* do," Etta said, looking from one woman to the other, "there isn't any problem, I guess. About this town of ours, I mean. About our being here."

They looked at one another.

"Put it this way," Miss Delfusco said. "*I'm* satisfied. Personally."

"And I am, too," said Mrs. Robinson. "Just between the four of us, the word I'd use is 'thrilled.'"

After that there was a silence in which both the women from the State looked down the street.

"But what?" said Mimimi. "Maybe I'm just being paranoid, but I could swear I heard a 'but' in there, somewhere."

That made it rueful smile time. The women's eyes came back; another set of looks went back and forth between them. Also sighs.

"Face it," Miss Delfusco said. "State regulations — I don't care what agency you're looking at — are rules that very cautious people made. . . ."

" 'Cautious' is a compliment," said Mrs. Robinson.

". . . to keep new things from happening. Things that might be 'dangerous'. . . . "

"In the sense of making work for someone," put in Mrs. Robinson. "People like the two of us, especially, the bureaucrats. We are the exceptions, please believe me." And she looked embarrassed.

"Almost anytime you find a program that's well-liked by kids," continued Miss Delfusco, "you can be pretty sure you're looking at a bunch of violations, too. The better liked it is, the more rules that it's breaking, probably."

"What she's getting at, I think," said Mrs. Robinson, "is that there are a lot of technicalities that could be raised about this town." She sighed again. "That *will* be raised, I guess."

"Just to give you an example," Miss Delfusco said. "If a legal 'child' is domiciled away from home, there must be a person in that domicile who stands *in loco parentis* — Latin, meaning 'in place of the parents' — who's, in effect, a legal guardian in case of some emergency. Like the headmaster of a boarding school would be. Who is that person here? That adult?" Her eyes went down the street again. "We've been told to have an answer to that question."

"For the files," said Mrs. Robinson. "*This* file, at least."

"Hell," said Miss Delfusco, "why not tell them, Mary Alice? We can flat deny we ever said it, if we have to."

"There really isn't all that much to tell," said Mrs. Robinson. She sounded weary, suddenly. "We were told to give this place a very close inspection. You can guess what that means, what that's shorthand for. Someone, for some reason, doesn't seem to want this town to stay in business. Not in its present form, at least."

"What you're going to have to put in all these-here," the Fire and Safety man explained, pointing at the row of different-sized, connected buildings up against the wooden western sidewalk, "is another means of egress from the second floor. Aside from jumpin' out a window." And he laughed. "*And* add your smoke detectors, up and down."

"Some sort of fire escape?" said Babe. "Like what you see in cities?"

"Hey, you got it," said the Maui-hatted man. "Of course, insteada metal, you could make free-standing stairsa pressure-treated lumber, like you see. You know the kinda thing I mean, I guess."

"Sure," said Seppy, thinking how long that'd take to do, unless they brought in lots of outside help. Materials alone would run into the thousands.

"Over there," the man went on, turning pages in

his loose-leaf notebook, "you've got a building that, in terms of code, is a hotel. Which means that with a frame construction and without no nearby fire-fighting aid, you need to install a sprinkler system." To clarify, perhaps, he held his right hand up and pantomimed some sprinkles with his fingers. "Sorry." And he shook his head. "Plus, once again, your smoke alarms throughout. I'm afraid the whole job's gonna cost you more than two new suits."

"Tell me this, about this 'code' you're quoting from," said Seppy. "When was that put in, exactly?"

"What? The building code?" the state inspector said. "Why, hell, the most of it goes back, like, fifty years or more, I'll bet. The smoke detectors now, I think that section just went in in '81 or '82."

"Then, how come all this time — "

The man put up his hand again, then flopped it forward from the wrist, three times. This time he was saying: Pipe down, just forget about it, kid.

"I know, I know," he said out loud. "What can I say? Out here in the sticks, you don't have all that many squeaky wheels or somethin' " — he turned the palm face up — "and so you don't get grease. You know how many guys like me there are for this entire *state*? I think it's thirty-eight, right now — and that's up three from last year — most of which will never go outside your seven biggest cities. You see what I'm telling you? I betcha here in Hupee County I could find a hundred violations in a day, for probably two weeks."

He fished inside his briefcase, pulled an Insta-matic out.

"Now, lemme see," he said, and aimed it at the

Armes. "Real quaint." Then he moved a short way up the street: an angle shot with mountains in the background. "Nice."

"No, no, no, no, no," said Sanitation, brusquely. "That's not the *point*. The water in the river there *is* cold enough; I grant you that. But streams are not 'refrigeration units,' as specified by code. For this number of people there's a specific number of refrigeration units that you simply have to have. You're getting the *effect* of a unit — several units — by keeping, say, those milk cans in the stream, but you still don't *have* the units that the code requires you to have."

He made an angry-looking check mark on a form. They hadn't left the kitchen yet, except for that small side-trip to the river's edge, but there were lots of problems already. Jake was looking pissed and Willa close to tears. The Sanitation man had found an ant; he'd found some open boxes of dry cereal, instead of just the single-serving size; he'd found the water temperature was three degrees too cool for doing dishes in the washer; he'd caught them harboring some crumbs inside the toaster.

And he'd told them that he must have maps or diagrams of all the septic systems in the town, in order to make sure the place was in compliance with subsection 84 of Act 493, which had only passed the legislature six short weeks ago.

If such maps or diagrams did not exist, he'd said, they'd better start in digging.

"Next on my list," he said with relish, fishing out another form, "is waste disposal, garbage. . . ."

*   *   *

218

"The trouble is," said Mr. Waxman, wearily, "the law is quite specific on the numbers deal. No more than *three* unrelated people can be domiciled together, except in registered hotels, motels, or boarding houses. *Or* boarding school and college dorms, or prisons and et cetera. But let me tell you this: As soon as you become, for instance, any one of *them*, then, Holy Columbus, you got a whole new *bookcase* full of other kinds of regs that suddenly apply to you. You see what I been saying? They get you coming and going."

Waxman shook his head; the state policeman nodded. Maria'd noticed that they did the opposite a lot. If Waxman smiled, the corporal would frown. When Waxman walked a little faster, then Mc-Queen slowed down.

"Jacks-'r-better is a *town*," the corporal said now. "It says so in the books. So, as a town, it must have records. We need to see those records. We need to see the voter grand list, assessments on all properties, and so on. We need the name of the town clerk, the constable, the registrar of graves, and other local officers." He grinned and nodded. "The registrar of graves," he said again, making sure this millionaire Maria knew he meant just that. He didn't like the E-Man's hair at all. It was pretty close to totally unstylish.

"Wait," Maria said. "The deed's on file in Hupee City, as I told you. What you call a town is *legally* . . . well, just my place, my ranch, my *home*. A lot of other ranches have a bunch of buildings on them. They're not towns."

"Quite true," the state policeman said, and grinned again. Mr. Waxman looked disgusted. "But according to statute the land you bought and the buildings on it are *still* the town of Jacks-'r-better. A town remains a town until the owner or owners of the land file the necessary papers with the Secretary of State at the capital. What follows is a hearing, after which — "

"Yeah, yeah, yeah," said Mr. Waxman, interrupting. "Legally, that's right. To be honest, it might be less trouble for you-all to go the other route and *be* a town. Have officers and so forth. Just something you can put on paper. The odds of anybody checking up on you are slim and none. The trouble is — "

"*We* know the situation now," the corporal said, triumphantly. "And that is one of noncompliance with the statutes." He started walking faster, heading for the Armes. They'd looked in all the buildings and then walked on out the far side of the town, so Maria could make clear to them exactly what she'd bought — where the "city limits" were. It was only twenty after three, but the corporal was hoping they could have this so-called "meeting" earlier than four, and hit the road. Things were pretty cut-and-dried, it seemed to him. Besides, state troopers got straight salary, no overtime.

Maria stayed in step with Mr. Waxman; she couldn't help but like the guy. They lagged behind, the two of them and E-Man.

"Look, I'm really sorry," Mr. Waxman said. "What you kids have going here seems good. My son, when he got out of high school, he was lots like you all seem to be. He needed maybe just a year, a change of pace, to look around a little. Get some reasons of his own for doing stuff, *you* know

220

what I mean. But we — my wife and I — we thought that if he didn't go right on to college, then he'd never go at all. You can guess what happened, right? He goes and pulls, like, possibly a one point eight, and wastes the whole entire year. And then he tells us that he's thinking of the Air Force, right? Well, hearing that we wised up fast, believe me. *Then* we asked him all the things we should have asked him, year before. Like, what's he really feel like doing? And you know what *he* said, which is what he's doing now? He said he wanted to build houses, working with his cousin, living in my older brother's house, back east."

He shook himself. "But that's not neither here nor there," he said. "You see the writing on the wall, I'm sure, as far as *this* town goes. And it's a shame. Believe me that there's not a single thing that I can do to help on this, 'cause if there was. . . ."

Maria wasn't listening. Her attention had been grabbed, and pulled way up the street. There was this bunch of people in a group outside the Armes. At first, she'd just assumed that they were hanging out, waiting for the meeting to begin, to hear what these inspectors had to say. Then she saw there was a strange *car* in the midst of them. And also — and incredibly — both Sookie and . . . (what *was* her name?) *Naomi!*

She'd read in books where someone's heart is said to "leap," and now that happened — *something* happened — in her chest. After which the gladness that she felt just made a wave, and surged, and broke right over all the gloomy stuff that Mr. Waxman had been saying. It was amazing, borderline impossible, but there it was. She felt like running up and hugging both of them.

But Roger, way up there, had seen her coming, seen *them* coming, and reacted. First, he faced the crowd, which seemed to pack itself around him when he did so. Then he turned and started trotting up the street in their direction.

He passed the state policeman, and kept on coming.

"Hey, Maria. E-Man," Roger said. Maria thought the way he slowed down to a walk and tried to sound so casual was just about the most absurd, transparent piece of acting that she'd ever seen. The cop had even stopped and turned around to watch.

"Could I just have a word with you and E?" Roger said to her. His voice was different, too.

"Sure," Maria said. She turned to Mr. Waxman. "Do you mind?"

"Abso*lute*ly not," the fat man said, and as the two of them veered off, he hustled to catch up with Corporal McQueen.

"Wait'll you see this," said Roger. He pulled the zipper for a pocket on the inside of one sleeve. "It's just about the worst bad news you could imagine."

"You found that Oreo you lost and it's . . . not well," Maria guessed.

"You've taken up guitar," the E-Man said, "and written me a song."

Roger made a face. He fished a piece of paper from the pocket — the map Naomi'd drawn with Sledge's route on it, the one that he was going to take to get to there, Mariasburg. The route that he had started on, already.

* * *

222

The next twenty minutes or so were a sort of a blur. Maria *had to* go hug Sookie and Naomi, first. Later on, the memory of that stood out, the moments she spent doing that. She used some words and so did they, but what they *said* was extra, didn't matter. Maria wept and laughed, both things at once; they all did, sure enough.

Seppy and the other guides were not that far away. They, too, got taken to one side and told. A few of them combined to get the state inspection team into the dining room, telling them the other kids would be right there, that they were picking up their *notebooks*, so they'd have a real good record of the stuff they had to do. Waxman and the women said they'd heat some coffee up, and maybe — yes! — get out those doughnuts that Maria'd mentioned.

The kids all came together, right there in the street; they numbered twenty-six again, with Sookie back and this Naomi in the group. Everyone agreed, in whispers: It was time to activate Plan B, for Bug-out. They'd grab what they could carry — a pack, their instruments — and jump on rafts and float and paddle out of there. Mimimi was sure her other jeans'd fit Naomi, so the two of them took off across the street. Seppy touched Maria on the shoulder.

"We'll be coming back," he said. His lips just barely brushed her cheek. "So, don't feel bad," he said. "Sledge really slipped his leash this time. He's gone too far. This ought to be the end of him."

She managed just a little smile. He was trying to help, and make her feel a little better. She knew he didn't feel that great himself, about a lot of things. Possibly including her.

"I know," she said. "I just feel awful for the *town*.

It's such a peaceful, loving little place . . . to get *invaded*." And she shuddered; couldn't help it. "Look. I'll tell the bozos from the State. We can't just leave them here, like sitting ducks. That Mr. Waxman's nice, and Mimimi said both the women — "

Seppy cut her off.

"No," he said, "let me do that. Really. You just head on out. Make sure that everyone gets on a raft. And then just leave me one, okay? Babe said there's extra — he kept changing the design." He pushed her shoulder. "You just go. I'll see you at the Lakeside Mill Marina." He looked preoccupied and angry, to Maria.

She grabbed his arm and pulled him close to her, and she kissed him on the mouth with great intensity. Then she turned and trotted down the slope toward the river.

29

Holed Up

As soon as Maria felt she'd gotten far enough away from the hotel, she left the path that headed to the river. Shielded by the trees and bushes, she cut behind the Armes and started up the hill again, heading for the street.

She reached it, checked in both directions, saw the coast was clear. She'd have to take the chance that neither Seppy nor the members of the state inspection team would now be looking out the lobby window. She was pretty sure the six of them would just be staring, open-mouthed, at Sep, while he strung out the story. It didn't seem like all that big a risk, that she'd be taking.

Go, she told herself. She sprinted at an angle, crossed the street, and ran up the sidewalk, to her room. She wanted Omar's shotgun. Although she didn't plan to ever use it, a major gun was something nice to have. Other people might be very much impressed by it, her having it, the way they might be by a diamond ring, or a diploma.

Once she had it safely in her sweaty hand, she waited, hidden, just inside her door, watching the hotel. Some minutes passed; she bit her lower lip.

At last the big front door swung open; out came Seppy. He looked both ways along the empty street, then turned and started walking briskly toward the river.

So it was time for her to move again. She burst on out the door, ran along the sidewalk, down off it and through the little parking lot, and up the other, longer, set of steps, and in the other door. That put her in the place she planned to stay, inside the church. For the duration, as they say, or possibly for good — whichever one came first.

She liked the building, lots. That helped. Inside, the church was clean and light, with big high windows and a high peaked ceiling. The trim was painted white, but the benches, fifteen rows of them, were warm, plain wood, sanded very smooth and rubbed with linseed oil into a nice soft luster-shine. Maria thought the room was down-to-earth and truthful. It was a place where she felt close to common and uncommon knowledge, both.

She ran down one side aisle and bounded up the six small steps onto the dais. She looked back once, one hand up on the lectern, remembering the day she'd almost stood there naked, thinking how that seemed like years ago. Then she took off again, this time through the little door on one side of the choir, up the narrow staircase to the steeple. She took the steps two at a time, until she got to Mimimi's small room, the one that Sook and Connie'd "borrowed," way back then. There she paused to take a few deep breaths and one quick look down through the peep-hole in the floor. She liked this bird's-eye view into the church below. The hole was right above the choir, and through it you could see the place from front to back, although from *in* the church you couldn't even spot the hole, the way the 'jacks had hidden it in scrollwork in the ceiling. Whoever rang the bell had had to have a hole so he would know just when to do his stuff, like at the end of services, or when the bride got kissed and headed for the exit. Maria'd wondered if the kid — she just assumed it was a kid — had ever had the urge to bomb the choir from up there. A drop of spit, say, or a worm, or maybe even spiders!

A moment later, she was up in her own special place, the crow's nest, with the trapdoor shut and the ladder she had used pulled up and safe beside her, and the riot gun.

As it turned out, she got there just in time to see the members of the state inspection team appear. It must have taken them a while to talk the situation over. How often, after all, could they have heard a town they'd just inspected was about to be attacked by a band of religious fanatics? Wouldn't there be statutes that prohibited that kind of thing? (They'd have to ask each other.)

Now, the six of them were talking, still, standing on the porch and looking up and down the empty street. Although she couldn't hear the words that anyone was saying, Maria caught some tones of voice. They sounded angry and upset, for sure. Clearly, there were different points of view about the situation.

Even as she watched, Maria saw the state policeman take (or, anyway, *assume*) command. His voice got louder and he gestured (crossly, thought Maria) in a number of directions. With that, the group dispersed. One, the Sanitation guy, re-entered the hotel, the others headed down the street and into other buildings. It looked as if they wanted to be sure the town was really empty. It wouldn't do for them to be the victims of a tasteless, childish joke. State officials didn't fall — or go — for stuff like that. Especially the ones in uniform.

Within five minutes all of them were back there on the porch again, shaking all their heads and making fresh suggestions. The cop looked even crosser. The trouble with civilians was they *always* had suggestions.

And then the first of Sledge's thunderbolts arrived. It was a mortar shell that arced out of the sky to land — as luck or skill would have it — squarely on the street, no more than forty feet behind where Sookie'd left her auntie's car.

Maria felt the shock of the explosion; she was sure the steeple swayed. She'd never seen or felt or heard a happening like that before. It made her wonder lots of things, pretty much at once. Was she right in thinking Sledge would never shell a church on purpose? And if she was, could she assume that he was good enough to always miss one? Well, she thought, this much was sure: If she was wrong, she wouldn't know that, consciously, for long. Now that she'd seen what his artillery could do — the crater that he'd made down in the street — she thought that any hit on any building there would pretty much destroy it and its occupants, if any. Like any steeple-jacqueline, for instance.

Reluctantly and cautiously, as if it were an unfamiliar snake, Maria pulled the fear that she was feeling out into the daylight, faced it. Doing that was scary, in and of itself.

Before, up there at Sledge's house, she'd also been afraid. But then she'd sort of had to fake it through. She wasn't in control back then; other people had her, *put* her, on the spot. This time, she had chosen her own spot. Nobody had made her stay, or climb up in a stupid steeple. Or lie there, wondering if maybe she'd get killed, at any time, for nothing.

For nothing? She had to ask herself that question. Suppose she *did* get killed, meaning she would never run or hug again, or tell a story, laugh, or eat an ice-cream cone. Sis and Mimimi and Seppy all would mourn her, she supposed, but would the *world* change any, with Maria dead? Would Sledge end up in any different kind of nuthouse, or would whoever had it in for this small town relent and say forget about the state inspection, let it keep on living? Would Omar never try to do a number on another girl? No, and No, and No, and . . . don't be silly.

She gave herself some moments feeling sad, acutely sad, about how little this Maria woman mattered, how really *insignificant* she was.

Except, she countered — wiggling her body on the mattress, feeling this Maria's front against the softness of the mattress and the inside of her clothes — except to this Maria. And that was part of why she wasn't going to leave.

This was her town, here. Not exactly her idea, but her ideal. Imperfect as it was in certain ways, it also served as proof, or evidence, that certain things were possible, or even *so*. Unless you understood about Mariasburg, believed in it (she thought), there wasn't any point in life, no point at all. It mattered in the same way freedom mattered, and integrity, and choice, and being true to who you are, no matter what, and love. *It* mattered, so did she.

So she was staying. She was going to wait up there till reinforcements came: the cavalry, whatever. That thought made her a little giddy; bugles in the distance, right? If she was hit, well then, so be it. Now, she didn't think she would be, but she let her lips move with the words "thy will be done." She'd always said that line ungrudgingly. It wasn't all that big a deal. If you believed in God at all, she thought, you had to think God's will made much more righteous sense than yours, for heaven's sake.

She was pretty sure that Sledge would never *occupy* the town. If he came down before the cavalry arrived, and he found that everyone was gone, he'd leave. It was only buildings, bodies he was after, not the concept. She would still be lying there, unnoticed and unconquered, in her town.

Across the street, however, there was no such faithful calm. When the mortar shell exploded, everybody froze, though not for long. The corporal recovered first. He made big shooing motions with his hands and arms, as if the other five were geese or chickens. They disappeared into the Armes again, maybe down into the basement, guessed Maria. But pretty soon the corporal appeared again. He ran, bent over, zigging left and zagging right, heading for his cruiser in the parking lot, Maria thought. But then he swerved and sprinted down the street, and up onto the wooden sidewalk, and Maria couldn't see him anymore. She guessed again: He'd want to call for help, and he'd remembered Jake's big radio — bigger than the one inside his car. And so he'd gone for it. Hooray. McQueen was going to call the cavalry to come and save a town he didn't even like or understand. He'd radio for them to send the cavalry, commandos, and maybe — if he had a kindly streak — a dozen easygoing orderlies with needles.

Now there was some movement back across the street, again. Maria watched the door of the hotel inch slowly open; out came Miss Delfusco's head. She did the standard looking-left-and-right. She saw what she had doubtless hoped to see: like, nothing. And so, now barefoot, she tore out of there and straight across to where her Mazda waited, followed very close behind by Mrs. Robinson, then Mr. Waxman and the other two. All of them piled in, the engine roared, the car shot forwards, backwards, stopped. Then, scratching blacktop madly, it sped off down the road, making what the five of them had almost surely called "a run for it."

Perhaps a minute later — she wasn't very good at estimating time — Maria heard what sounded like a rifle shot go off, and then another, then a lot in rapid sequence, which then slowly tapered off to just a few, then none. Maria thought she heard the car, still, for a while. Then nothing. Back to silence.

Corporal McQueen appeared again. He ran into the middle of the street and stood there looking down it, hands on hips. Maria knew he also didn't see a thing; *she* couldn't, from a much, much better vantage point. But McQueen still held his ground, his pose: Lawman in the middle of the street, in empty, little, failed-inspection town. Lawman looking to be challenging the bad guys. Let them come on in and make his day.

Another shell arrived and landed in the brush

behind the first house down from the hotel. Another huge explosion. The corporal rocked slightly, then looked up, and taking one hand off one hip, he raised it in the air to shade his eyes. A moment later, he was running toward the hotel porch, still looking back and up, the way a baseball fielder might, tracking down a long fly ball.

Maria searched the sky and didn't see a thing. She heard some car-sound in the distance, though. Could it be Relief, already — and spelled how? No, that was impossible. Too soon. It seemed to be approaching, coming fast. She heard a single shot, but that was it; there weren't any more.

The car roared into town and stopped. Maria stared, a little goggle-eyed. It was the sheriff's cruiser with its windshield fixed, and there, behind the wheel, that Omar. She touched the shotgun on the mattress next to her. He'd given her permission, hadn't he? Of course, she knew that he was way, way out of range.

The state policeman ran out on the street; Omar left his cruiser. They stood there talking in the middle of the street. When they finally started walking toward the wooden sidewalk, it was not too fast. Neither of them checked the sky; they'd bought the macho package. They went together up the sidewalk steps; Maria couldn't see them after that.

Another shell exploded, this one on the church side of the road, a little way behind her sanctuary. Maria swiveled on her belly and saw the cratered gash that it had made there on the hillside; there was some smoke around the edges of the thing. Another huge explosion followed, seconds later, this one just behind the place Maria's room had been,

232

halfway down the row of houses on the sidewalk. She thought McQueen and Omar were in one of them, talking on the radio again.

Maria got up on her hands and knees and turned back facing the hotel. And just in time to see, she thought, a consequence of that last bang: the trooper, in his squad car, peeling out of there. His Dodge had great acceleration, but after he'd been gone a little bit, there was the sound of shots again, one of them a real big boom. Afterwards, however, there was still some car-sound; maybe Sledge and them were not that great at warfare after all, Maria thought. Omar hadn't come back into view.

Maria waited. She sat up on the mattress now, the shotgun cradled in her lap. The less that she was taken by surprise, the better she would like it; that's the way she viewed the situation. She didn't see or hear a thing, other than the normal and ex-pected sights and sounds: some birds, a rush of wind, the river. The peacefulness of all of that was almost shocking.

And then there *was* an unexpected and unwel-come noise, the sound of footsteps. They were on the steeple staircase, coming up. She heard the latch click in the room below, footfalls coming in. A pause, and then the sound of something being dragged along the floor. It had to be the heavy table there, the one that Mimimi had kept some books on, and her notebooks and her sketch pads and pastels, and pens.

Soundlessly, she raised up Omar's riot gun and held it in both hands, clutched against her chest. She looked down at the barrel of the thing, then stared at the trapdoor. She could hear the person climb up on the table; she knew exactly when he'd start to straighten up. She could tell what he was doing, almost see him doing it — Maria with her X-ray vision, superchild. She also knew what she was going to have to do, assuming that he kept on coming. Given who she was, she didn't have a choice.

There came a little knock-knock-knocking on the trapdoor; it hadn't moved at all.

"Mya? Hey, Maria. Open up, it's me."

He kept his voice real sweet and low, that Seppy did.

30

Steeple People

Hearing Seppy, *seeing* him, made Maria cry. She didn't make a big production of it; Omar, after all, was still around, somewhere. Her sobs were more like little liquid hiccups, mixed with "oh" and "Seppy" sounds and meaning, mostly, she was glad he was alive to love, and with her in her world at all.

Seppy just assumed he understood. He didn't cry, but once he'd got the trapdoor closed again, he held her very, very tightly, and pretty soon he kissed the wet spots on her cheekbones, and her lips. After some of that, she smiled and looked at him and shook her head in wonder. Relief was surely in the picture, too, somewhere.

"How come. . . ?" She had to know.

"When I got down there, to the river, Mimimi was waiting by the rafts, with Sookie and Naomi. She said you hadn't showed; she thought we were together. We both knew where you'd be. Meems wanted to come back with me. I talked her out of it," he said.

"You think I'm crazy, probably," Maria said.

"Of course I don't," he said. He reached and

smoothed her eyebrows. "I think you're being totally Maria. This is just the sort of thing that girl
would do."

He smiled. Maria couldn't tell if he was hating
. . . well, that *side* of her, or what. Putting up with
it in spite of . . . or because. . . .

"But you're here, too," she said. "Is that like
Seppy — being here?"

"I guess it must be," Seppy said. He ran an open,
testing palm across one cheek, his chin, and up the
other cheek. "Seems I haven't broken out with hives
or anything. I guess I'm not allergic to the whole
idea."

"Let's see," Maria said. "We'd better run a thor-
ough check." *Play*, she told herself, just play along.
Make it like the good old days, the way it used to
be. It maybe was a little strange, to sit there talking
spots and allergies instead of gee-our-lives-are-both-
in-danger-aren't-they? But what the heck, what
wasn't strange, *mysterious*, this side of Mamacita?
Or any other side of it, in fact. The marvelous and
main thing was: He had come back. She went ahead
and pulled his shirt out, and started to unbutton it.

"You get the rash down on your stomach first,
a lot of times," she said. "That's common knowledge, right? I'll check it out, if you'll just give us
your cooperation, sir."

He raised his eyebrows, shrugged, rolled over on
his back, beside her on the mattress. She undid all
the buttons, spread his shirt out wide.

"Well," she said, "it looks as if he's telling us the
truth, nurse Piggy. Smoother than old Noah, not a
single spot. If anything, I'd say he *loves* it here, going
by the front he's putting on." She bent and kissed

his stomach, said, "Mmm-*hm*. That's just a fact. He's perfect." Everything felt different, now that he was there.

"See?" he said. "No problems with *him*. I was pretty sure there wouldn't be. He's just a plodder, kind of like somebody's loyal hound dog, pretty much the same, day in, day out. Our doctor, she's a different story, though. Recently, she's sure been acting strange. Almost as if she'd gotten to prefer a *place* to any *person*. Not to make a real big *thing* of it, or anything."

She was lying on one elbow, watching him. He'd framed what he was saying with that smile of his, and turned away, but she could tell that he was serious. She knew she'd hurt him badly. Not meaning to, but still. So, there was stuff he had to hear from her, right then.

"Oh, Sep," she said. "I'm sorry. I'm sorrier than slime. I never felt that way inside, not even for a minute. But me, I'm such an idiot, I didn't tell you — show you — what I did feel, did I? Nowhere near enough, at least. There never would have even *been* a town without you being with me." She ran a fingertip along his jawline. "Everything I do is so tied up with you," she said, "I swear I even *feel* the same as you, a lot of times" — she paused — "impossible as you may think that is, given how I've acted, lately."

"Well, I don't know," said Seppy, sitting up. His face had changed, his tone of voice. He does too know, Maria thought.

"*Feel* the same as me?" he said, and he was teasing, like the old days, now, with everything all tight and warm around the edges. "You? Maria? A member of the royal family? Erstwhile Queen of Pizza? Well, I doubt that very much."

"In that case. . . ," said Maria. And so — Her Craziness — she undid all the buttons on *her* shirt, and smiled, and slipped it off her shoulders. "I guess you'll have to check the situation out yourself."

There was a cool, fresh breeze against her breasts. She more or less could tell how she was looking, kneeling on the mattress now, in the slanty brilliant light of afternoon. Way up there with him, she felt as if the two of them had found a new dimension. It had a size and shape unique to them and their experience, and no one else could see or even know of their existence in it. And so to take her shirt off there, or not, just didn't matter. The fact was it was done, and simply done, and done to make them happy. They made up the dress code, here.

"Oh, gee," he said. He was looking at her in a way Maria loved him to: her Seppy. She knew, once and forever, that he understood.

He came to his own knees and put a hand around her neck, another on one breast. His mouth was buried in her hair, just above one ear.

"You don't feel *anything* like me," he whispered. "You're a hundred million times more beautiful. And good. You're so incredibly damn good. Me, I'm just a selfish jerk, expecting you to go on taking care of me, as if there wasn't anybody else that needed you. I'm the one that's sorry, Mya. Sorry every way there is."

Maria'd got her mouth on his, by then. She hadn't had to hear all that to know that they were back together, all the way, and so she let herself go-drift in rapture, loving how his hand felt on her breast, the strong familiar feeling of his lips, the Seppy taste and smells. *Good*, she thought, is what he is, just purely good. And loving him is lots of what it's all about.

But, weirdly, wanting him so much and being all that conscious of how good they were together — those things suggested action and brought back the other world, where people fired guns and otherwise assaulted one another. And where making love made babies if you didn't plan ahead of time.

She groaned.

"Mya," Seppy said. He'd taken his great hand away and now was looking in her eyes. Smilingly, and knowingly. As if he'd read her mind, or maybe sent the message. He knew the world was too awash in accidents, already. They'd had a pact on accidents, forever.

"Our luck," she said. She wrinkled up her nose to show she didn't really mean it. "The perfect place and person comes along, but then . . . and anyway. And so. . . ." She reached behind her, grabbed her shirt.

"Just in case," she said. She put it on and grinned at him; her heart was beating hard. Still. "I'm guessing Sis'd rather that they found me fully clothed. I mean the searchers-through-the-ruins, not ol' Sledge and Omar."

She barely got that out before the next shell landed, this time, for the first time, on a building. On the furthest house away from them, in fact, one of two on their side of the street, beyond the row of houses that their rooms had been in. Solidly as it was built, the little boxy-looking place was mostly blown apart, and some of what was left began to smoke.

"Oh, Lord," Maria said. "D'you suppose this means he's got the range?"

Seppy saw the next one hit, this one on the next house closer, on its small porch roof and it, that house, was also instant rubble, totaled.

"It's looking really possible," he said. Their hands moved left and right along the mattress, found each other.

Maria bit her lip. Now she'd seen what Sledge's guns could do to buildings, she felt a little sick. Staying there and taking chances with herself was one thing; having lovely Seppy there was quite another. He'd never leave her side; she knew that just as sure as she knew Sis remembered rolls and butter. So, if she left, he'd certainly go, too. She wondered what was going through his mind, right then.

Actually, Seppy was thinking that perhaps he'd have to move her. As in, pick up object M and then, ignoring any kicks and screams, carry to location B. No, wait. Maybe, first: Unload extremely dangerous weapon G, before proceeding with step one. Or, possibly, be sure that weapon G is fully loaded; learn to brandish same.

Then he thought: Where *is* location B, for Better? Come up with one example, please. He'd seen the sheriff's cruiser parked down in the street. Was *anywhere* with Omar better than this steeple here, without him? Probably, he thought, they ought to just stay put.

"Maybe," said Maria, "we should take the elevator down and am-scray out the back, as Sis would say. But, trouble is, there isn't any *door* in back. Or any elevator either, come to think of it." She knew that she was babbling.

Another mortar round came down, and then another, causing them to flop face-forward on the mattress. Both the shells, it seemed, were aimed across the street. One took out the furthest building there; the next one, closer, landed in the street. The pair of ruined houses on their side were burning briskly, now.

"It starts to look as if he wants to flatten the entire 'burg, from one end to the other," Seppy said. "And if *that's* the plan. . . ."

"What I've been counting on is that he'd spare the church," Maria said. "That a guy like him'd never blow a *church* apart." She felt a little shaky, saying that.

"Hmmm," said Seppy. "Well, *you'd* know, I guess. I mean, he's more *your* friend than mine." Shaky as she was, she swatted him. And felt a slight bit better.

There was another boom. They got a lot of shock from that one; the steeple seemed to sway, again.

"Oh, damn! Oh, *shit!*" said Seppy. "He hit *my* place, the bastard."

That was a fact. The shell had landed in the row of houses fronting on the wooden sidewalk, right where Seppy's room had been.

They looked at one another. Maria found her eyes had filled with tears. Seppy's room. That was a special place. Another shell came down across the way, squarely on the house beside the Armes. Sledge was going to blow the town apart; that much was getting obvious. He was going to punish her. He'd told his family it was the Lord's idea (or so Naomi'd said), but she, Maria, knew that it was personal. Sledge was out to beat her, one way or another. She was both a woman and a child, and not a true believer, so she was going to get it, Omar or no Omar. She felt a crummy, helpless rage well up inside her.

"If I had a gun, I swear...," she said, out loud, and Seppy looked at her. She *had* a gun. If Sledge were there, right now, would she shoot the thing and try to kill him? Seppy didn't think so. But still, he totally endorsed the feeling.

"Here we are again," she turned and said to him, still furious; tears were streaming down her face. "they're *doing* it to us. Just like they always have. They won't let us alone, even when we go a hundred miles away. Another bunch of them — "

He put his arm around her and a finger on her lips. She realized her voice had gotten much too loud. And worse, it was a *victim's* voice, a little bit hysterical. That made her even madder, for the moment. That wasn't her, no way.

She sucked a deep breath in and tried to make the anger and self-pity take a hike. Neither one would make the situation any better. How it was was how it was; call it "life," or possibly "reality" (oh, no — Maria thought). Everyone was equally exposed, at risk. A person might get hit by love or fame or fortune — or by loneliness, or poverty, disease. By craziness, like Sledge, or by a mortar shell, like she and Seppy might be. Or one from Column A and two from Column B, or vice versa. Not all of that seemed *fair*, which left: *So what?* Or, once again and better yet: *Thy will be done.*

Seppy was looking at her. Sort of anxiously, she thought.

"I'm okay now — again," she said. She even got

242

a smile out for him. "But don't you maybe think we ought to head downstairs? Part way, anyway? We wouldn't want to miss a chance to split. Like possibly if Omar leaves, or something. All we'd have to do is make it to the river." She wondered if she really meant that.

"I don't know," he said. "I wish I knew where Omar *was*. Then, maybe. . . . *Uh*-oh. *Look!*"

He didn't have to say that; she was looking.

31

Shooting Star

Omar still was dusty, slapping at his sleeves, a little bit off balance as he hit the street. He'd been just four strong, solid walls and maybe forty feet away from Seppy's room when Sledge's mortar shell dropped into it. The blast had knocked him off his feet and rung his bell, but good. Fuckin' crazy man, he thought. The three words occupied his mind and stayed in it, blinking like a neon sign: *Fuckin' crazy man.*

He hadn't needed any part of this. For openers, he hadn't needed news that there were people from the state up there, splashing in his private little pond. But even more he hadn't needed what he'd found when he'd arrived, this Sledge, this fuckin' *crazy* man, acting like the Lord of Hupee County. It was bad enough that he'd attacked Mariasburg without so much as giving him a call — without a single "May I?" But now, to top it off, he'd come within *that much* of wiping out the one man in the world that Omar really cared about. Never mind the Armageddon crap; this deal was really bad already. And could get much, much worse. And then move on to *catastrophic.*

When Omar'd first got into town, and saw and heard what kind of stuff was going down, he was *at least* relieved to learn the kids had gotten out of there, and no one had been hurt, *so far*. And so, at once, he'd tried to talk the pansy cop, McQueen, into a second message to the capital, saying local law enforcement was on hand and in control — canceling his Mayday call for help, in other words.

That hadn't worked. McQueen was acting like an asshole, calling Sledge's people "insurrection-ists" and "militant subversives" and "an outlaw *army*," for Pete's sake. It seemed as if he wanted more, not less, "support." An MX missile or a Min-uteman or two would probably have been just peachy keen.

But once McQueen had left the scene (to "help direct the operation from the zone's periphery," he'd said), Omar had some hopes of getting Sledge dispersed before the "operation" started. The point was simple and compelling: Omar didn't want old Sledge in *anybody's* custody, not even his. Crazy as a coot or not, the guy could sing some songs, for instance one called "Me and My Sweet Sheriff," maybe. That one wouldn't make the charts, but surely would send *him*, the sheriff in the title, off to one bar-windowed room with meals and clothes provided by the state. For entertainment, there'd be games of Kick (the former lawman in) the Can, he'd bet. That wouldn't be enjoyable at all, and there'd be other games they'd want to play with him that would be much, much worse than that.

So, the fact was simply this: He had *got* to get the guy dispersed, or else.

"Or else get killed myself," he muttered to himself, still dazed, but out there in the street.

There hadn't been another shell, he didn't think. Not since the one that knocked him down and almost out. Maybe Sledge was wising up. After all, he knew where Omar was; he'd seen him driving toward the town. He wished *he* knew where Sledge was — not just in general; exactly. It'd take a while to find him in the woods, and he was running out of whiles. No, he thought, the thing he'd have to try to do was bring Sledge into town, to him.

Omar took out his revolver, held it pointing right straight up, as if he was the starter at a track meet. He squeezed off three spaced shots, then paused, then fired three more times. He then reloaded, standing in the middle of the street, and put the gun back in its holster. He wanted Sledge to see him by himself, to know there wasn't anyone in town but him. He took out his pocket handkerchief, thinking that perhaps he'd wave it once or twice. But that meant "truce," not "I'm alone down here, come down." It also possibly could look a little wimpish.

And so, instead, he took a leak, legs wide apart, standing in the middle of the street. That ought to get his point across, he thought.

A little over seven minutes later, Omar heard the sound of motors, small ones, not well muffled. And pretty soon he saw what made the sound, coming fast in his direction: three 3-wheeler ATVs. Each one had two riders, all in camouflage fatigues and bristling with weapons; it was Sledge and Josh and Enos, along with Sledge's oldest sons. They came in like the German army coming into Paris, grinning ear to ear. They also circled Omar once before they skidded to a stop.

"I am the voice of someone cryin' in the wilderness," Sledge hollered (not bothering with " 'Afternoon," or "Howdy"), "an' I not only make the Lord's way straight, I also make it *flat*, if I've a mind to." And he cackled.

" 'Tall cities are reduced to plains an' ash heaps, and the unbeliever's flesh is shamed and mortified, but good,' " he said. "*I* said all that. If the great Jehovah and myself had so ordained it . . . well, this little town would now be history. Nonex*istent* just as Sodom is, wiped clear out like naughty ol' Gomorrah."

He looked from left to right, expectantly. Omar didn't move or speak.

"Now where's that girl Maria and the rest of 'em?" Sledge asked. "She's still got business with the Lord's anointed, Sheriff Omar. Even if she's turned to salt, she's gonna take a lickin'." And he laughed again.

Omar tightened up his lips and laid some hard-stare on the guy. It was time to cut the crap. Past time.

"You dope," he said. "Those kids are long since gone. They're out of here, they're history. And if you've got the sense God gave green apples, you'll be the same, damn quick. There's going to be some people showing up before — "

"What?" cried Sledge. He knit his brow and cocked his head right over to one side. "Gone? They can't be; that's impossible. There's just two cars gone down that road, the little-bitty red one and that smokey's.

You mean they've gone into the woods? Well, then I reckon we can have ourselves a rabbit hunt — right, boys? Bag ourselves a bunch of little cottontails."

"They aren't in the woods," said Omar. "They went on down the river. While you were playing with your popguns there, and staring at the highway, they were getting on a bunch of rafts and floating off as pretty as you please. By now, I bet they're down there at that Lakeside Mill Marina, playing games of shuffleboard or something." Omar *sneered* the last of that, as best he could.

"What?" said Sledge, again. His face was getting red. "They floated down the goldang river? There isn't anybody in this town at all, excepting you and us?"

"Exactly right," said Omar. He pronounced each word with extra clarity, like an angry parent speaking to a child. "This town has emptied out and, like I said, unless you want to *die*, or go to *jail* from now until the twenty-second *century*, you'll head not only out of *here* but, soon as you can pack it up, out of this whole *county*. But now, before you go, maybe you could tell me why in hell you didn't stick to our agreement and just let me — " He broke off suddenly, looked up, and stared in horror.

"Damn! Damn! Damn!" he screamed. "And *now* just look what's happening!"

He pointed. Tried to think and point at once. Decided to stop pointing and begin to shake his fist at Sledge, instead. It was possible some fellow had a 'scope up there. Shaking-fist'd give the right impression, Omar thought, when seen from up there in the sky.

That time of day, above the town of Jacks-'r-better, the sky was largely empty, as a rule. Oh, sometimes there'd be buzzards or a raven (and Roger recently had bought another kite to fly). But never, never *this* before. What the sheriff and those six Defenders of the Fate were looking at was totally unprecedented.

The thing that Omar didn't realize — how could he and why should he, after all? — was that the governor had panicked. When he had got the word that out of all the towns it could have been throughout the state, this Jacks-'r-better had come under mortar fire, he'd pure and simple flipped. There was a person in that town, the son of an electrical contractor, who, if money talked in politics (and he believed it did) he simply had to save — protect. Or seem to, anyway. And so he'd lunged at his red phone, and as soon as it was answered, be'd begun to order out — and not Chinese or pizza. This was exactly why there was a Guard at all, he told himself. In wartime, they were national, the U.S. President commanding; but otherwise they were a state militia, sort of, there to help preserve the *status* of his *quo*. The nice part was: He'd get the Guard down there and let whatever happened happen. He wouldn't be involved directly. But if it worked out well, he'd take the bows.

And so, the sky that afternoon above the town of Jacks-'r-better (sometimes called Mariasburg) contained no less that fourteen military helicopters, as well as six big-bellied transport planes, from which there soon began to shower parachutes.

Sledge, Josh, Enos, and Sledge's eldest sons looked up in awe at this display of state (and federal) armed might. Although they didn't acknowledge either of these governmental entities as having any jurisdiction over *them*, they could still be stunned, *impressed*, by what they'd (in a sense) begat.

"Je-*hos*ophat," said Josh, distinctly. Enos also spoke, but what he said, his words, were even less familiar.

Omar was every bit as awed as all of them, but being many times less faithful, he was also much more worried. How in hell could he get out of this? The guardsmen weren't after *him*, he knew, but still. He thought, again: If ever they got Sledge wrapped up and talking . . . well, forget it.

Sledge had put a carbine to his shoulder and had started shooting at the choppers. It looked as if the guy was having fun. Josh and Enos and the boys saw that, and grinned, and did the same. It *was* fun, they found out. The helicopters quickly veered away. As far as Omar could determine, they were more the transport kind; in any case, they didn't open fire on his group. *Possibly* because they saw his uniform, thought Omar. The parachutists were descending all around them but they, by accident or plan, were slightly out of range, although the guys kept potting at them also, merrily enough. What he and these six lunatics were damn soon going to be (the sheriff thought) was totally surrounded.

He really didn't see that he had any choice. The thing he had to do was not his sort of thing — his style — at all; he much preferred to use his mind, psychology. Guns were crude, a kind of last resort, but he was clearly at exactly that, a last resort. And it wasn't a Club Med, or Acapulco. He couldn't

250

stand there, doing nothing, and simply let his whole career go down the tubes now, could he?

Omar had his piece, his pistol, halfway out of its black leather holster when good old Sledge — the crazy man — acting on some impulse of his own, crouched and whipped around, said "Judas *Priest*," and put a rifle bullet squarely in the center of the sheriff's star.

32

Getting the Word

Maria and Seppy saw the shooting, plain as day. Omar was blasted back and spun around; he landed on his side and lay there in a lifeless heap. It could have been a dummy in a uniform; he didn't even twitch.

Because they couldn't see a wound, or any blood, or even Omar's face, the scene was far less shocking and disgusting than it might have been. In fact, Maria had to say, in whispered awe, "He's *killed* him," before she understood exactly what she'd seen.

Then she felt a wave of nausea sweep over her. She'd feared and hated Omar, but the wish that he was dead had never made it to her heart, she realized. And now the man was dead (like, *dead!*), and Sledge, who'd killed (yes, *killed!*) him, and his sons and friends, seemed pretty unexcited by that fact. They all were looking at the body pretty much the way they'd look at any other piece of road-kill. They were talking back and forth, but not excitedly; one of them, a younger one, stuck out a toe and kicked at Omar's pistol, got it farther from the body.

"Cripes," said Seppy, softly. "Just like that."

Maria kept on staring at the body, at the other

six. The nausea had passed and now — already — she was getting slightly used to what had happened. She remembered how she'd felt when she had thought that it was Omar in the steeple, coming up and coming for her (she'd believed). She found that part of her was . . . well, *relieved* that he was dead. That she wouldn't have to be afraid of him again. Right away, she felt ashamed of her relief, but still the feeling didn't leave her altogether.

"Boy," said Seppy. "Look at all the Army guys. When they come to save a little town, they sure don't kid around."

Maria pulled her eyes away from the group around the body. She saw what Seppy meant. The guardsmen were closing in from all directions. She thought that there were *hundreds* of them, all completely uniformed for combat, and carrying, or hauling into place, all sorts of lethal weapons. Rifles and machine guns were most common, but she also thought she recognized bazookas, flamethrowers and mortars, also long-nosed antitank guns, along with other kinds of cannons.

"Good grief," she said. "They've got enough stuff there to fight another *country!*"

Seppy nodded, equally amazed himself. Before he answered her, however, a single shot rang out from up the slope behind the church. The six men in the street all spun around, and looked in that direction.

"OKAY, LAY DOWN YOUR ARMS AND RAISE YOUR HANDS." The rapid-fire, amplified, high-pressure salesman's voice boomed out from more or less the place the warning shot had come from. "YOU ARE COMPLETELY SUR-ROUNDED BY UNITS OF THE 28th DIVISION,

AIRBORNE, U.S.A. RESERVE, R.G. RAINTREE COMMANDING. YOU'LL NEVER GET A BETTER DEAL THAN THIS ONE, MEN. LAY DOWN YOUR ARMS AND RAISE YOUR HANDS AT ONCE, AND YOU'LL BE GUARANTEED A FAIR AND SPEEDY TRIAL. YOU HAVE THE RIGHT TO REMAIN SILENT AND NOTHING THAT YOU SAY WILL . . . UH, RESULT IN ANY CRUEL OR UNUSUAL PUNISHMENTS. AND THAT'S A PROMISE FROM R.G. RAINTREE, COLONEL, 28th DIVISION, AIRBORNE, U.S.A. RESERVE. JUST PUT THOSE ARMS RIGHT ON THE GROUND AND RAISE YOUR HANDS AND WE'RE IN BUSINESS."

Maria saw Sledge scratch his head and look around. Then, all at once, he started running toward the church, still carrying his rifle, sure enough.

"BullSHIT!" he yelled. "You can't try us, or even lay a finger on our clothes. Not when we got *sanctuary*. Goddam it, boys, come on! Come on and get yourselves in sanctuary. *Sanctuary!*" He screamed it louder still, in the direction of the voice from up the slope.

"All houses of the Lord are sacrosanct!" he hollered, sprinting up the street. Presumably, the colonel and his troops looked on in sheer amazement. In any case, there weren't any further shots. "Woe to all defilers of the holy places. Whoever shall besmirch a church and not respect the rights of sanctuarians shall first be split and skewered and then charbroiled under the licking tongues of flame." He bounded up the steps, the others close behind him.

"That's *everlastingly*, you bastards!" he bawled out as his amen. They disappeared inside.

Seppy and Maria looked at one another. If Omar's shooting had been unexpected, horrible, this development was nothing less than staggering. The two of them were now together in a church, along with the most dangerous and militant members of The Defenders of the Fate, all of them surrounded by the U.S. Army — or at least by the National Guard, units of the 28th Division, Airborne, Colonel R.G. Raintree, U.S.A. Reserve, commanding.

And, as they watched, the guardsmen started slowly closing in from every quarter, with their weapons pointed at the building. One shot by Sledge or any of his men (Maria thought) could set off such a salvo in return that the whole church might very well collapse around the ears of the Defenders. And part of all that falling rubble would be she, herself, ex-Queen of Pizza, and her former consort, Seppy.

Maria racked her brain. Maybe they should try to hail this Colonel Raintree from the steeple. But the soldiers, nervous and perhaps not *too* experienced, might jerk their guns right up and shoot at them. Or maybe they should go on down the stairs as far as possible so that, in case the soldiers rushed the building, or fired tear gas in, they could just get captured with the other ones, and then explain things later. Or maybe they should try to *write* a message they could *throw* down from the steeple. Maybe they should just. . . .

Maria closed her eyes and gave her brain a rest.

Seppy sat there, watching her. He, too, was trying to think. He was sure that soon this Colonel Raintree, U.S.A. Reserve, and probably real used to fast, decisive action in civilian life (wasn't there a Raintree Cadillac in Mamacita?) would order tear gas lobbed inside, at least. Or, possibly, he'd try to start a fire in the church and smoke them out of there. Ideally, he'd want to find a way to make old Sledge and them lay down their guns without a lot of shooting, first. That way, if any of those boys were ever thinking of a Cadillac. . . . But Seppy felt the chances of that happening were poor; in fact, he thought that wouldn't happen. Sledge was just too crazy.

Maria opened up her eyes and smiled at him. Seppy's heart rolled over, wagged its tail. She was just so beautiful, so wonderful. She mustn't — couldn't — die inside this funny little church in rural Hupee County. This couldn't be the end of her, him, them — Mariasburg.

Maria didn't *look* like someone who was going to die, at all. Instead, she looked serene and confident. She rose now, to her knees, and lifted up the trapdoor, very carefully.

"Wha — " Seppy started, but she put a finger to her lips and smiled again.

Moving slowly and, once more, with careful concentration, she stood and picked the ladder up, put it down the hole and got a foot on it.

"Stay here." She mouthed the words at Seppy, barely breathed them. "I'll just be right down there." She pointed at the room below.

"There *is* a way," she said.

He nodded — watched her slowly, step by step, go down the ladder. She looked as if she knew what she was doing, as if her mind was flat made up, as well. It was the look that she had gotten on her face when she had told them, months before, about this town that she was going to have, that all of them were going to have, forever.

When Maria reached the bottom of the ladder, she turned and tiptoed straight across the room. When she was right above the peephole, she sank down on her knees.

Down in the church, below, Sledge had drawn his forces up for battle — or that's the way it surely looked to her. All of them but him were kneeling on the front row bench, facing toward the rear, with rifles resting on the bench's back and pointing squarely at the church's double doors. Sledge himself was standing right behind the doors, peering through the crack between them.

He turned and faced his men.

"They're all out there, all right," she clearly heard him say. "And you won't believe the stuff that they got pointed at us. They must have known what they were up against, I'd say."

Maria heard what sounded like a muffled sob.

"Hey, don't you worry, boy," Sledge said. He pointed at his youngest son. "No call to whimper, now. The six of us got sanctuary. We're under His protection. There's no way we can die in here. You'll see."

Maria knew there'd never be a better time than then. She bent way forward, so her lips were almost in the peephole.

"*Sledge,*" she stage-whispered, portentously — and paused. "*Oh, Sledge,*" she said again, and quickly pulled her mouth away so she could see down there, again.

Sledge was staring upward, staring at the ceiling

of the church. He looked a lot the way he had back in that special room, back in his own big house, except he now looked (also) utterly amazed, aghast. The other five were doing just the opposite of him; they'd sort of curled up into balls and bowed their heads.

"Where is my prophet, Sledge?" Maria, bent back over, asked in what just had to be the very much most queenly tone that ever passed her lips.

Sledge's eyes got even wider, looking upward. His face was ashen, now. His head was twitching, giving small, astonished shakes.

At last, he found his voice.

"Yes, Lord," he said. His eyes blinked rapidly. "Here I am, right here. Your servant, Sledge."

"Well, this is what you now must do. . . ," Maria said.

About the Author

JULIAN F. THOMPSON didn't move to a ghost town to explore his vision of reality. His passionate and controversial novels are written in Vermont, where he lives with his wife, Polly, who is a painter and designer. His other novels include the award-winning *A Band of Angels, Simon Pure,* and *Discontinued.*